Storyteller's Note

Question: What on earth am I doing writing a book about a pig living secretly with a working-mother chef, her two children, and a cat in a four-star hotel in New York — instead of telling a tale about islands, ships, and planes?

Answer: Swine not?

— JIMMY BUFFETT

Also by Jimmy Buffett

A Salty Piece of Land

A Pirate Looks at Fifty

Where Is Joe Merchant?

Tales from Margaritaville

(AND FOR YOUNG READERS)

The Jolly Mon

Trouble Dolls

JIMMY BUFFETT

Swine Not?

A NOVEL PIG TALE

Illustrations by

HELEN BRANSFORD

BACK BAY BOOKS
Little, Brown and Company
New York Boston London

Back Bay Books / Little, Brown and Company
Hachette Book Group
237 Park Avenue, New York, NY 10017
Visit our Web site at www.HachetteBookGroup.com

Originally published in hardcover by Little, Brown and Company, May 2008
First Back Bay paperback edition, May 2009

Back Bay Books is an imprint of Little, Brown and Company. The Back Bay Books name and logo are trademarks of Hachette Book Group, Inc.

The characters and events in this book are fictitious. Any similarity to real persons, living or dead, is coincidental and not intended by the author.

Special thanks to Nina, Lynda Lou, Amy, Sunshine, Karen, Kathy, and Bonnie for shepherding me along through the whole pig-tale adventure.
I couldn't have done it without you. — J. B.

Photograph on page xiii by Benjamin Mendlowitz
Photograph on page xxi by Pamela Jones Photography
Photograph on page 16 by Julie Skarratt

Library of Congress Cataloging-in-Publication Data
Buffett, Jimmy.
Swine not? : a novel pig tale / by Jimmy Buffett ; illustrations by Helen Bransford.
p. cm.
ISBN 978-0-316-11402-8 (hc) / 978-0-316-11405-9 (pb)
1. Manhattan (New York, N.Y.) — Fiction. 2. Domestic fiction.
[1. Pigs — Fiction.] I. Title. PS3552.U375S95 2008
813'.54 — dc22 2007050612

10 9 8 7 6 5 4 3 2 1

RRD-IN

Printed in the United States of America

For Jane Buffett,

who knows how to put people

and pigs together in the same pen

Always remember,

a cat looks down on a man,

a dog looks up to a man,

but a pig will look a man

straight in the eye and see his equal.

—Winston Churchill

Contents

About This Book

SOMETIMES YOU have to find the story, and sometimes the story finds you. In all my previous fiction, the stories were rooted in this nomad life I live. I converted my real-life experiences into fictional fun and made up a few more tales myself — always keeping a bit of mystery as to what was based on reality and what had sprung from my imagination. Faulkner said he was a liar by profession, and he made good money at it. However, in the case of *Swine Not?,* the story came to me.

One day our friend Helen Bransford brought over a manuscript she had written and some illustrations that went with it. She asked me to look at them. I knew the basic story, and everyone who knew Helen did, too. Her real-life story was this: Former Belle Meade debutante from Nashville, Tennessee, winds up marrying well-known author and moves into the Carlyle Hotel in Manhattan with her husband, twin kids, cats, and large pet pig — which she conceals from the management for two years. I had joined the chorus of Helen's friends who had told her, "You have to write this stuff down." When you're a fiction writer, you sometimes simply can't top the facts.

It is a unique and magical thing to read an original story for the first time, especially when what you are reading is good and, in my case, makes me laugh out loud. Those original twenty-five pages of text and the accompanying illustrations hooked me. The idea of a mom and two kids hiding a pig in a four-star hotel suite on the Upper East Side of Manhattan got me thinking. When I finished reading Helen's story, I walked from the office to my house with a smile on my face. I told my wife, Jane, who had introduced me to Helen many years earlier, that this was one of the quirkiest and funniest stories I had read in a long time.

The next morning, just before sunrise, I made my cup of English breakfast tea and walked out of the silence of the house into the still-dark morning. My usual route was down to the dock to smell the sea, then up the oyster-shell driveway to my office to work. My job that morning, I thought, was to edit Helen's story and give it back to her with my advice about where to get it published. That would take me into midmorning, and I would drop off the manuscript at her house on my way out to surf.

Lindbergh said, "We are of the stars," and I believe and feel it and have always looked up to them for guidance, whether I was trying to find my way across the ocean or into the yet unwritten pages of a story. Standing at the water's edge, I took in the view overhead of lingering planets and constellations still visible over the bay. My front yard, where the sea meets the sky, combined with the silence and the beauty of the natural world at that hour of the day, has long created a thinking spot. Sometimes there are things in a story or a song that need to be worked out. Other times I am just waiting to be struck by some invisible asteroid of inspiration. It is a good way to go to work, especially when you don't really know what your job is.

Well, that morning, the stars did not directly do their inspirational thing, but instead they pointed me toward another source of thought. Sitting fifty yards off the beach was my little sailboat, *High Cotton*. She was a lovely and, some say, historic little gaff-rigged sloop that looked as good sitting at rest on a mooring line as she did under full sail. The sun was just beginning to light the sky to the east, and there was barely a whisper of breeze on the bay. I could hear the water, pushed by the incoming tide, lapping against her hull. As I sipped my tea and savored the moment, it suddenly happened. The stars had come through again. Staring at *High Cotton,* I heard a chord of familiarity ring out, and the universe connected the sailboat to Helen's pig tale.

High Cotton was not a name I would have chosen for a boat, and it certainly didn't fit the list of past vessels that I had christened. She had been someone else's dream, and someone else had named her. Naming, and especially renaming, a boat is a very serious and superstitious undertaking. It would be like renaming your child. Somewhere back in the mythology of mariners, it was decreed that if you acquired a boat that had already been christened, you could rename it only once, and the moment to do that was immediately after you sailed her for the first time. If you did it any time after that moment, it was very bad luck, and nobody wants to sail on a bad-luck boat.

When I bought *High Cotton,* she had come with an incredible pedigree, having been designed by Nathanael

Herreshoff as a Buzzards Bay 25 and having been built at the legendary Brooklin Boatyard in Maine by Joel White, master boatbuilder and son of E. B. White. In her first year, she had made herself an instant reputation as one of the fastest and most beautiful boats in New England, and had won prestigious races from Newport to Nantucket, but I had not bought her to race. All I was looking for in *High Cotton* was a beautiful single-handed boat that I could spend time in alone on the water. With all the other things that I find myself doing, I still just like being a sailor best, and sailing a boat alone is what a good sailor can do. *High Cotton* may not have been my original idea, but I could make her into that kind of boat and stay true to the designer's original vision.

Staring at the boat that morning and listening to the stars, I realized that, like *High Cotton,* Helen's pig tale was a treasure I had inherited. It had captured my attention and had gotten me thinking that there was more to the story. That is the way I felt about my little boat.

In its original form, Helen's manuscript was totally entertaining and funny, but it also contained the potential for many characters and plots I was curious to explore. With Helen's permission, I wanted to customize her boat. I called her later that morning and asked what she thought of my ideas. She laughed, and in the spirit of good fun, she let me loose; I was off and running to my imaginary shipyard.

I headed to the office, reread the manuscript, and started thinking about who and what I could add to the pig tale. It didn't take long before I was working out new plotlines. My plan for the story was not to change course but to add some interesting stops on the journey. I was sailing into uncharted waters as far as pets were concerned. The only pets I have ever owned were dogs. I take that back. I did own a parrot for one day, but I returned it to the pet store after the parrot made it very clear to me and my valuable thumb and forefinger on my left hand that it did not desire to be part of my life. I knew nothing at all about pigs as pets. I was about to find out plenty, and now so are you.

There are many people out there who have funny stories to tell, but it's the writing-it-down part that's tricky. I can tell you that even though writing is a gift, it is not one that comes with a set of instructions or an autopilot. You wonder why a lot of writers go crazy, drink themselves to death, or become recluses? Because it is hard work! I know. I could never have guessed that this little piggy would end up taking more than two years to write, but I should have known from my experience with real voyages. As Billy Cruiser says in an earlier book, "The best navigators are not always certain where they are, but they are always aware of their uncertainty." Longer-than-expected voyages come with the territory if you truly are a sailor. The journey can go on a lot longer than you expected.

As I said before, sometimes you look for the story, and sometimes it comes to you. So if you are asking yourself the question "What on earth is Jimmy doing writing a book about a pig instead of about boats, islands, bars, ballads, and beaches?" the answer is simple: "Swine Not?" I hope you enjoy this story.

— JIMMY BUFFETT
NOVEMBER 5, 2007
PALM BEACH, FLORIDA

Apology to the Author

Mr. Buffett, I apologize for trying to shove you into the fireplace the day we took photographs at Helen's house for the book. It was not my fault. I wasn't being territorial with your space on the sofa. I was just hungry, and you happened to have been sitting on my favorite snack. What can I say? My genetics took over, and I guess I should tell you, though it is after the fact, that you should never get between a pig and her favorite food. That said, I look forward to working with you on future projects. Oh yeah, I am also sorry that I bit you.

Sincerely,
Rumpy

Swine Not?

CHAPTER I

Don't Look Down

Rumpy the Pig Speaks

I think there comes a time in everyone's life when the werewolf-like winds of misdirection and the beasts of bad timing put us in an impossible situation. In my case, the question was this: How did a 151-pound pet pig manage to live undetected in a four-star hotel in New York up until this very moment? And what was a pig like me doing, shivering on the ledge of the hotel roof, twenty-five stories above Fifth Avenue?

"Don't jump," I heard a voice call out.

"I have no intention of jumping!" I wanted to reply,

but I was too scared to move, much less carry on a conversation. The ice beneath my feet gave no quarter. The wind howled and swirled above my head. I prayed that I wouldn't be turned instantly into an iceboat sail and be sent over the edge – for it was a long, long way down.

"Don't jump," the voice repeated.

I had no idea where it was coming from, and I did not dare look down. The skyline of Manhattan was at eye level and bobbing like an apple in a tub. The trees of Central Park bent and swayed in a fierce wind. The noise from the busy avenue below me would block out any attempt I made to squeal for help.

I did not sign up for this kind of trip. Pets rarely do. Our owners just assume we want to go along, and we often find ourselves riding off into the sunset with the excess baggage, iPods, cell phones, and Igloo coolers that belong to our well-intentioned but misinformed masters and mistresses. Pigs are not allowed in four-star hotels in New York City. Somebody should have thought about that before they brought me here.

If only this ice could melt beneath my short, trembling legs. Perched on the ledge, minutes away from turning into a very porky Popsicle, I would have given anything for a local news crew in a helicopter to hover above my chilly head and send some caring soul to rescue me.

A sudden gust of wind slammed into my side, and I did the only thing I could — I stiffened every muscle in my body and resisted the force with all my might. I was as rigid as one of the statues in Central Park across the street. It seemed like an eternity before the wind finally subsided, but I still couldn't relax a muscle. And then I saw the tiniest bubble of hope arch above the trees. The survival corner of my brain blared out a warning: *Don't look down! Don't look down!*

I sucked in a gulp of fresh air, and for an instant, it was void of the telltale scents of the millions of city animals, plants, and machines I had come to know so well. I ignored the flashing red warning light in my brain, and I let my head tilt ever so slightly down past the ice-covered ledge, down over the trail of taxicabs creeping up Fifth Avenue to the spot where the ball had landed.

"Don't jump," the voice called out again.

I was both scared and relieved that someone was watching me, but my eyes were now fixed on that ball as it hit the ground. It was not a falling star, a meteor, or one of a thousand things that could fall out of a New York City sky. No, it was a soccer ball, and it instantly reminded me of where this whole story started, in a much more peaceful place called Pancake Park in a much smaller and quieter town called Vertigo, Tennessee. . . .

CHAPTER 2

Coach Mom

Barley the Boy Speaks

"This is a soccer game, not a civil war!" our coach shouted to the opposite side of the field as she wiped blood from the nose of a girl lying across her knees. Her words were aimed like missiles at a middle-aged man in a blue jogging suit with MOONWALKERS stitched across his jacket. Standing on the sidelines with a clipboard on his potbelly, he was smugly nodding his hearty approval that one of our players had been injured.

My twin sister, Maple, ran up with an ice bag, and our coach administered it on the spot. She was a woman who could handle an emergency. I should know – she was also my mom.

Connie, our goalie, was able to stand again in a matter of minutes but was in no shape to continue playing. "Barley McBride!" Coach Mom shouted in that tone I knew so well. "Time to get Rumpy!"

"Vait a minute! Vait a minute!" the Moonwalkers coach barked as our substitute goalie trotted onto the field. "Vhat is dis? *Svine?*" He led his team in a chorus of laughter, ridiculing our goalie as she waddled toward the net.

"She's our substitute goalie, that's what!" Mom replied, thrusting a copy of the roster at the referee beside her.

"Maybe you vant to forfeit now, before da ham sandvich humiliates you."

"Feel free to get a ball past her, Colonel Klink," Mom shot back.

The referee studied his folder and then pronounced, "The pig is on the roster! Get her in the goal. Moonwalkers won the toss and will kick first. Five shots per team. Let's go."

The Moonwalkers were the undefeated bullies of our soccer league. They were sponsored by the Cadillac dealership in Huntsville, Alabama, where they had their own sports complex. We, the lowly Moccasins from Vertigo, Tennessee, were sponsored by a hippie shoe store and played on a simple field called Pancake Park, the only flat surface in town. It was shaped like a giant footprint, as if some monster stuck his big leg out of a cloud and stomped one of the many hills that surrounded Vertigo.

The Moonwalkers featured an all-American goalie whom our local soccer world called Spiderwoman. Six feet tall, with arms that could reach across the goal, she had gone seven games without allowing a score. But that day her record had been broken – by me. The furious Moonwalkers coach began screaming on the sidelines, and his team responded. They came roaring down the field with a vengeance, sending Moccasin defenders flying. They had taken out Connie, our goalie, in the process of tying the game. Now we were headed for a tiebreaker with the "Goonwalkers," as we called them.

Our pet pig trotted all the way to the end of the field, sporting a custom-made face mask to protect her tender snout. My sister had designed it. Rumpy took her place in front of the net as the opposing team continued to laugh their heads off. Like everyone else, they underestimated her abilities, and it would cost them.

Spiderwoman was back in form and made four dazzling saves, but Rumpy was just as brilliant. She knocked every shot astray of the net. The last striker for the Moonwalkers approached the ball as if he were going to kick it into low earth orbit, but at the last minute, he lobbed a high, arching shot. A collective gasp came from the Moccasin players and fans. They watched in horror, knowing that our goalie (who stood all of two feet, eight inches high) was far beneath the rainbow-shaped path of the final ball.

Agony turned instantly to ecstasy as Rumpy somehow bounded skyward and put her front shoulder between the net and the ball. It bounced harmlessly out-of-bounds.

Seconds later, I put a nasty spin on the final shot and collected my second goal against Spiderwoman. We won the game and were crowned champions of the Alabama/Tennessee Coed Soccer League. Next thing I knew, I was on the shoulders of my teammates, and Mom and Maple were dancing in a circle with Rumpy and the rest of our fans. Manny Brown, the owner of Manny's Moccasins Shoe Store, accepted the trophy, and we shook hands with the Goonwalkers as they shrugged by us, mumbling, "Good game."

The coaches were at the end of the line. My mom

extended her hand to the opposing coach, but he walked by as if she didn't exist. I knew Mom, and I knew something was going to happen. You did not insult her or her pig and expect to walk away unscathed.

She waited for the man to put some distance between them. Then she dropped the ball she was carrying. "Hey, Adolf!" she yelled, and as the man turned toward her, she let go with a wicked shot that sailed just above the ground. Steadily it rose until it hit him, as the TV announcers say, "directly in the groin."

"That's for the bloody cheap shot at our goalie," she said as she watched the man rolling on the ground in pain.

"Vait until next year," the man gasped. "I'll get you for zis."

"I doubt that you'll have the chance," Mom said.

That night, after the party in the pizza parlor, I asked Coach Mom what she meant by her last words to the Moonwalkers coach.

"Oh, nothing," she replied casually. "Just another one of my wild ideas."

In that synchronistic blink only twins know, Maple and I were instantly on the same wavelength, thinking collectively that when Mom said "nothing," she really meant "something" – and we smiled.

CHAPTER 3

Learning to Play the Angles

BARLEY

I REALLY HATE voice mail. That's what I get when I call my dad to tell him about a game. He calls back, of course, and he always promises that one day he is going to take me to see my favorite player, Darryl Meacham, who plays for Real Madrid in Spain. But by the time he calls, it is past both my bedtime and the initial moment of glory that I wanted to share with him. Dad is usually several time zones away from Tennessee.

As usual, I left him a detailed message about the game

and the goals. I also told him about Mom's little post-game stunt. I knew it would make him laugh.

I used to get real mad about Dad leaving, but that is how I became such a good soccer player. At first, I took my anger out on the ball. I would kick and kick and kick until I thought my leg would fall off. Then I started getting good and began kicking with both feet, and then I started to figure out the angles and how to make the ball go where I wanted it to go. It all helped me deal with the feelings I had about my dad.

Another good thing I learned is that soccer is not a one-man sport. It is a team sport, and you have to depend on, and get help from, strangers. After you help them or they help you, they become your friends. Along the way, you also figure out the angles to the goal, which aren't that far from the angles of life – even in a town named Vertigo.

The New York Red Bulls are my favorite team, and I hope to play for them when I'm old enough. I was born in New York, although I don't remember much about living there. I was only three when I left. So how did a future striker for the New York Red Bulls end up in Tennessee? To quote the title of a country song by Tammy Wynette, it was "D-I-V-O-R-C-E." Back in the ancient days of the 1970s, when the song was popular, a family with just a mother and kids was called a "broken home." Today it is referred to as a "single-parent family." Either way you slice it, it is still only half a loaf.

My dad, Oliver McBride, was an English teacher from Boston. He moved to New York, where he met my mom, Ellie Dean. She was a former beauty queen from Clarksdale, Mississippi, who was in culinary school. Though my dad was a fine teacher, he had this pipe dream to be in the movie business. One summer, he got a job as a script consultant on a gangster movie that was filming in Greenwich Village. That was it for the academic world. He quit teaching and started hanging out with other would-be actors and directors, drinking lots of coffee and talking about what they would all do when they got famous.

He and my mom dated for about a year while he wrote his first movie script. They were part of a wild crowd back then. After a party, they ran off to Haiti and got married, and it was only upon their return to New York that my dad learned that not only did my mother come with a steamer trunk full of handed-down Southern family recipes and a closetful of debutante gowns, but she also carried the barnyard gene. This manifested itself in her immediate acquisition of a mean dog, a dozen chickens, a cat, and a baby potbellied pig, whom she scooped up one Thanksgiving back in Mississippi. She somehow managed to stuff all of them into a rental apartment in Greenwich Village. My dad thought he was marrying a Southern belle–turned–city girl, but what he really wound up with was a circus act.

After we were born, we were celebrated at many a party. The champagne flowed, and once our parents actually left us in the restaurant under a table. We were quiet babies; the adults made most of the noise. Space was the first problem, and then the issue was money. The mean dog went to the police-dog program, the chickens went to live on a farm on Long Island, and my dad made his first — and last — sale of a movie script.

The movie business doesn't appear to have a lot of financial security. That didn't seem to matter to Dad. He went from being a writer to a producer, but not much was produced. Meanwhile, Rumpy and the cat stayed, and they seemed to get more of my mother's attention than my dad did. That is when he took off for Hollywood, promising to become rich and famous. Then he planned to return to New York and lather us with luxury.

That didn't happen. Even at three years old, my sister and I could pick up on it with that "twin thing." My earliest recollection that our lives were changing was when my sister and I had to start sharing our desserts with our pig.

I love my pig, but food is a big deal to a three-year-old, especially dessert.

Somehow my mom managed for a year, baking pies and pastries at a fancy diner, but living in New York ain't cheap when you're a petting zoo. One day, a registered letter arrived at her door telling her that her old aunt Margaret had just died and willed her a farmhouse in Tennessee. A week later, she found a job at the famous Opryland Hotel, and we went south, where we have been ever since.

My dad actually did kind of make it in Hollywood – not as a filmmaker but as a copywriter for commercials. Plagued by Catholic guilt, he tried to make up for his lack of availability by helping to fix up the farm in Tennessee.

Dad is presently in Alaska doing a dog-food commercial and working on his sixty-seventh screenplay. All but his first have been rejected. Still, he keeps trying. I guess that once the movie-business bug bites you, you live with the sting. I love my dad, but his accidental fall through the looking glass of Hollywood has warped him. Dad loves us, and he gets along with Mom as long as we all fit into his pattern. I think he sees us, and all other humans for that matter, as bit players in his imaginary films. It never occurs to him that other people might see him as a stand-in in their own movies.

CHAPTER 4

Raising Humans Is Hard

Rumpy

My name is Rumpy. As you can see, I did not go over the icy ledge, and it's a good thing because you wouldn't have gotten my side of the story. Living with humans is not easy. They have quite an opinion of themselves, but few of them seem to be playing the game of life with a full deck. How about that "ham sandwich" crack by the Moonwalkers coach? Well, Ellie made him pay for that one. It's a lot different in the animal world. We don't come with emotional baggage. I'm simply Rumpy, the pig who saved the game. It's not the first time I have been called from the sidelines.

Since you have heard Barley, the soccer jock, give his version of the family, now I will give you mine. Despite all their human weaknesses, I adore them, and they adore me. At bedtime, the twins argue over whose room I'll sleep in. Maple arranges my coat with a brush while Barley rounds off my hooves and gives me tummy rubs. Then Maple braids my tail. They bathe me once a month, dab me dry with towels, and cover me with rose oil to keep my skin soft. They love me so much.

I came into their lives as a baby and really don't know any other home. I have a twin brother who – you may find this hard to believe – is even smarter than I am. He now lives a thousand miles away in New York. It has been many years since I have seen or heard from him, but something about being twins keeps us connected. His name is Lukie, and I have missed him terribly ever since we were separated.

To remove another stereotype, I am not a barnyard animal. I prefer the comfort of the farmhouse to the farm. My favorite place is Maple's closet, where I go for afternoon naps. Unfortunately, Barley is a neat freak. The first thing he does after a game is *wash his uniform!* Maple and

Ellie . . . well . . . I really hate to use this term, but it does apply here. They are such *pigs*. Barley's bedroom always looks as if he is prepared for a surprise inspection by a drill sergeant. Though I respect Barley's neatness, I *love* Maple's closet. Her corner of the world is filled with piles of books, CDs, fashion magazines, and an abundance of outfits she creates for her dolls, her friends, and herself. That girl is into fashion, and if she isn't studying designers on the Internet, she is cutting, stitching, and sewing, which makes for quite the mess. It never feels lonely with all the outfits and pieces of clothing dangling over my head – long and short, dressy and plain. Those twins are a huge responsibility for me, but it's gotten easier since they turned twelve. We are just about the same age, but in pig years, I am the adult around here. In one more year – maybe two – I'll have them fully trained. Next come the teenage years, and what happens then is anybody's guess.

That brings us to Ellie Dean McBride. Now let me start off by saying that the math in this family has pretty much been minus one in the man department during and after her only marriage. She is the poster image for single mothers of the world, raising two kids, coaching soccer, working at the Opryland Hotel, caring for a farm full of four-legged creatures – and then there is the catering business that she created and runs out of an old smokehouse behind the barn. I don't see how she does it all, but she does.

The only real problem any of us ever seem to have with Ellie is her rare, quick flare of temper that sometimes has long-lasting effects. Take, for example, her well-aimed soccer-ball shot at Coach Goonwalker. But, I guess, when you think of all Ellie has had to put up with, she deserves to give life a kick in the butt every now and then.

To her credit, with all the literal and figurative plates that she has spinning in the air, her kids have turned out pretty well so far. Not having a full-time dad around is not an easy way to grow up. The twins seem to think of him more as an older brother away at boarding school than as their father. They have accepted the fact that his e-mails, cell-phone messages, and occasional souvenirs from far-off lands qualify as sufficient parental participation here in the twenty-first century.

CHAPTER 5

Instant Replay

BARLEY

"MOM'S GOT a date!" Maple beamed. "Maybe she was just warming up for a male encounter at the soccer game."

This was big news around our house. With the exception of Dad's unpredictable and unscheduled "pop ins," there hadn't been a lot of eligible bachelors "comin' a courtin' " around the farm.

"She met him on the Internet!" Maple added.

"Oh my God!" I was shocked.

"What's wrong?"

"The Internet . . ?"

Maple rolled her eyes. "Would you rather she was looking for Mr. Right in a Hooters outfit, pushing hot wings? Women do it all the time, Barley."

"I just thought she was done with dating," I said.

"Her married girlfriends talk about it all the time, and the Internet is easier and safer than a singles bar."

"When is this big date supposed to happen?" I asked.

"Tomorrow night," Maple told me. "In fact, we are going out this evening to buy a dress. I'm planning on making her spend some money on herself and buy an outfit by Karen Wu. You want to come with us?"

Maple was obsessed with Karen Wu, one of the top fashion designers in New York. Her picture and photos of her creations were taped all over Maple's room.

"Let's see. I think I have a root canal scheduled after supper."

Maple threw a pillow at me.

Rumpy and I watched from the porch as Mom and Maple drove away. Mom looked very excited. I had grown accustomed to only seeing her in jeans and checkered chef pants and soccer shorts for as long as I could remember. I was happy for her.

LATER THAT EVENING, Rumpy and I were half asleep on the couch, and in the background I could hear the voice of Mario Batali coming from the TV as he explained the ingredients in a tartar sauce dip he was mixing on the *Iron Chef*.

"Wake up and read this," a voice whispered loudly into my ear. I felt a nudge and opened one eye. Maple was standing over me with our cat, Syrup, draped around her shoulders. She was holding a handful of printed pages. There was no mistaking her seriousness.

I sat up, pushed Rumpy off my leg, and rubbed my eyes.

"I Googled Mom's blind date. He's not so blind anymore. You better check it out."

Maple disappeared into her room, and I looked at the color photo on top. The headlines made my jaw drop. My mom was going out with a *football coach*.

CHAPTER 6

Men Are Not Pigs

RUMPY

OINK! WELL, Syrup the Cat isn't the only four-legged creature around here with a streak of curiosity. I, too, was awakened by Maple's loud whisper, and I subtly opened one eye. Then I read the pages Barley was spreading out, one by one, on the couch between us.

They say a picture is worth a thousand words. The first page had a large photograph of a smiling man with a preacher-politician grin. It spoke loads about cosmetic dentistry and plastic surgery. One could only wonder what was really behind that huge, reconstructed smile. I read on. Oh yeah, in case you didn't know, some of us pigs do read.

The second page was composed of clippings from the Nashville paper, hailing Coach B. A. Boykin as some kind of messiah. He was a local ballplayer who had made the big time in the NFL and was now joining the Titans, our Tennessee pro team, as its new head coach, heralded by headlines, photo ops, and muffler commercials.

Like Barley, I am *not* a football fan. I had been exposed to the game far too many times in Pancake Park. Soccer is an afterthought in Vertigo, and Pancake Park had been groomed, manicured, and designed primarily for football, which is still looked upon as religion in Tennessee. When fall comes, battalions of leagues, from peewees to tiny mites to midgets to players from elementary schools and Vertigo High, take over the park and do battle. I think there would be a league for babies in diapers if some fans around here had their way. We soccer nerds take a very distant backseat to this kind of football madness.

The next page dropped in front of my snout. "Oh no," Barley gasped. It was a story Maple had downloaded from a feminist Web site. The title of the article was "Women Beware: The Twenty Worst Eligible Bachelors in America and Why You Want to Avoid Them." The story led off with Coach B. A. Boykin and his years as a pro quarterback with the Arizona Cardinals, his born-again experience, and his run for Congress. There were pictures of him deer hunting and playing golf with George Bush. Barley and Maple went off to search the Internet for more, so when I had read enough, I ate the pages, climbed off the couch, and went outside for a walk. Then I curled up on the rug by the porch swing for a nap.

I dreamed about Lukie and the time he rescued a little boy from a flash flood. I could sense that something big was in the air, and it had to do with Lukie. I could feel it.

My dream woke me up. It was dark, but the blue glow of the TV screen upstairs lured me inside. Ellie and the kids were watching ESPN *Sports Center,* and I cuddled next to them while Ellie scratched my head. On the screen was the now-familiar face of Coach Boykin, but he was not coaching. He was seated behind a huge set of drums made to look like football helmets. The interviewer was not focusing on football but on the fact that B. A. Boykin also played in a local country band.

"Not a bad drummer," Ellie said, looking to all of us for some kind of approval of her date.

None came.

"Time for bed," Ellie said. We all did as we were told. Tomorrow was going to be an interesting day, and we needed our rest.

CHAPTER 7

Down on the Farm

Rumpy

If the Hummer painted to match the eye-popping blue colors of the Tennessee Titans wasn't enough, it was what Coach B. A. Boykin was carrying in his hand that freaked us out the most. You would have thought that, on a first date, he would be holding flowers or a box of chocolates. But no, when he planted those boa constrictor–skin boots in our driveway and stepped away from the car, he was carrying a football – autographed to Ellie! Do you know the slang term for a football? *A pigskin!!!*

The kids were standing next to Ellie and me on the porch. When prompted with a nudge from their mother, they walked forward to meet their guest. Syrup, who had been lying limp as a dishrag on Maple's shoulder, suddenly sprang to life on all fours. The hair down her backbone stood up as she locked her cat radar on the man with the football. Then she catapulted from Maple's shoulder to the nearby low-hanging branch of a pecan tree and didn't stop climbing until she reached the highest limb.

"You a Titans fan, hotshot?" the coach bellowed to Barley.

"I'm a Red Bulls fan," he replied.

"Me, too. Used to mix the stuff with vodka back in my drinking days before I found my Lord and Savior, Jesus Christ."

Barley looked stunned by the coach's first words to him, but the game had just begun.

"I mean the soccer team in New York," Barley told him.

"Never heard of 'em," Coach replied as he twirled the football in his bear-paw hand. "Know what we call those soccer-style kickers in the NFL?" He answered his own question. "Kangaroos!" His pronouncement was followed by an uncontrolled laugh. Then the six-foot-four man dressed all in black pointed his finger down the driveway and said, “Go long!”

“Me?” Barley asked.

“Yeah, you!” Coach shouted.

Barley shot a glance at his mother. She smiled at Boykin and motioned Barley down the drive with a slight wave of her hand. Off Barley trotted toward the barn, looking back at the man with the ball.

Barley has made known to me his feelings that football is a violent game played by men on growth hormones. He cares as much about football as he does about earthworms, but off he still went.

The ball sailed from the coach’s hand, spiraling skyward. Barley calculated the trajectory of the falling pigskin and ran toward it.

“Arms out in front of your body! . . . Extend those hands!” Coach bellowed.

Barley tracked the ball, but his arms remained at his sides. He measured the rate of fall and positioned himself under the ball. Instead of following the coach’s instructions, he used his left foot and stopped the ball inches from the ground. Then he kicked it up so it landed on his head, then dropped it back to his foot, and with a powerful kick, he launched the pigskin in the opposite direction – over the picket fence and halfway up the hill, where it disappeared into the branches of an oak tree.

"You're supposed to *catch* it, son, not *kick* it!" Coach yelled out from up the driveway.

"In Europe, they call *soccer* football!" Barley yelled back.

Ellie met Barley halfway down the driveway. With a stern hand on his arm, she directed him to the fence. "That's enough, mister. Go find Mr. Boykin's ball," she said in her strictest coaching voice — the one that signaled she meant business.

"It's a present, and you can call me B.A.," Coach called out.

Ellie hesitated, and then she answered, "Right."

At that moment, Sissy, the teenage babysitter, cruised up on her Vespa, and Ellie pointed her toward the kitchen. "Sissy, there is a quiche in the oven for supper. We are going to the movies, and I will be back at ten. Barley, you find that football. Maple, get the cat out of the tree, and then help your brother."

The coach assisted her in the climb that was required to get into the Hummer. She looked lovely in her new Karen Wu dress — graceful and elegant beside the screaming colors of the hideous Hummer. As we watched Coach walk around to the driver's side of the mammoth vehicle, he stared straight at me. I recognized that familiar look of disdain in his eyes and knew right away that he envisioned me only as the main ingredient in a BLT – not as a member of the family. Then he roared down the driveway, spraying pebbles on the lawn.

The kids did as their mom asked and searched for the ball under the big oak tree at the edge of the woods, but with very little enthusiasm. Sissy called out from the house that supper was almost ready. That was all the excuse the twins needed to call off their search. They darted for the house, leaving me alone in the woods.

It was hard not to follow them; I wanted a slice of quiche, too. But something made me stay, and it was not Ellie's command that kept me searching. There was another reason I had to find that football, but I wasn't sure what it was. Soon I would know the answer.

CHAPTER 8

Ghosts in the Trees

Rumpy

Things are very vertical in Vertigo, and I was never one of those pigs who liked to run off exploring and rooting around in the brush. Most of the time I left the eerie woods around the farm to the badgers, raccoons, and foxes that I would see darting at dusk across the open pastures to their hiding places. Barley had told me about the ancient Civil War trench that circled the hill behind the barn. He and his friends still occasionally found rusty minié balls and Confederate uniform buttons in the dirt.

No, I didn't like these woods at all. I could sense that a lot of humans had died here in that Civil War time. Still, I was determined to find the football, and sometimes a pig's got to do what a pig's got to do.

I knew the ball was in one of three places – the trees, the trench, or the creek. The moment I started to climb up toward the tree where the ball had gone in, I was huffing and puffing. It was made worse by the scent of quiche baking. I blocked the aroma of grilled onions and bubbling cheese from my brain and hunted on.

There was no sign of the ball in the trees above. That was good news, and I rummaged forward until I saw a berm snaking around the hill. It had to be the trench, and it would surely have stopped a ball from rolling down the hill.

I felt the sadness of the loss that occurred here as soon as I stepped in the trench. The way I heard one of Barley's friends tell it, in one afternoon's battle, three Confederate generals and nine hundred boys were killed. They were buried by the woman who owned the land – and then she wrote a personal letter to the parents of each boy. Places of death are not popular in the animal world. During the French Revolution, there were so many executions that the smell of human blood sent animals fleeing.

These woods were like that to me, and this trench still held a lot of the past. There surely were ghosts in the trees, and when the sun dipped behind the hill and nighttime came, it was a place I did not care to visit. I quickened my search along the trench but neither saw nor smelled the football.

Strange thoughts often are strongest in strange places, and I began to think that if I could find the pigskin, it might be an omen that was meaningful in my search for my lost brother. Lukie and I were just babies in Mississippi when he left home for New York City. It took a long time for me to understand that his sense of adventure and exploring were early signs that he had special work to do. Mama told me he would be happy and thrive in New York — where people really needed his help. And then I moved in with Ellie and Oliver in Greenwich Village, excited and hopeful that I would see Lukie one day. But instead I was whisked away to Tennessee, where I have been ever since. I never saw Lukie again, though I had picked up several "scent-mails" over the years, like those rogue radio signals that bounce off the atmosphere.

Scent-mail, if you're wondering, is the way communication has evolved in the world of pigs. I can't speak for any other species, but we pigs can't Google. We have no fingers, but our snouts are the numero uno search engines in the animal world. We are able to smell the breeze like nobody else. Not only can we find food but we can locate friends, family, and a whole lot more. Pigs have been sending scent-mails ever since we were loaded onto that overcrowded ark, which wasn't exactly a Carnival cruise. But, like those radio signals and satellite-TV transmissions, scent-mails do have their limits.

As the sun began to set in Vertigo, I had my head down and my snout to the ground, sniffing for clues. I was thinking more than smelling when – *wham!* – the scent of the ball was in the leaves. I was on the trail. I spun around and thrashed at the earth with my hooves, sniffing for more. It took only a few seconds, and I had it again. I charged like a wild boar in the direction the scent was leading me.

I was out of the trench and back in the woods when I ran full steam into a big boulder in the middle of a field. It knocked me for a loop. The next thing I knew, my short legs flew out from under me, and I was squealing and rolling uncontrollably down the hill and into the creek. I lay there, out of breath and motionless, the whole world spinning, but somehow, through all the confusion, I could still smell leather. When I managed to stand up, the final rays of the sun were lighting up a patch of the creek, and there, sitting among the river rocks, was that pigskin.

The aches and pains of my tumble immediately disappeared, and I raced to it with joy. I grabbed the laces in my teeth and hurried home.

I did not take the football to Barley and Maple but hid it in the back of the barn, where I had stashed a few more treasures. A girl has to have some good-luck charms, you know. Anyway, despite the way the football came to me and the original horror I had felt when I first saw it, I now realized it actually was a sign. It had been punted into my life by the ghosts in the trees to remind me of someone I had lost a long time ago and hopefully would find again. That night, before I went to bed, a shooting star streaked across the Tennessee sky. I made an instant wish. Little did I know that my wish would be granted the next day.

CHAPTER 9

Uprooted Like Truffles

Barley

When I woke up, I was thinking about that kick. I did hit it perfectly, and a football is much harder to kick because of its shape. I lay in bed, daydreaming that it was a sideline shot in the Major League Soccer finals for the Red Bulls.

Mom wasn't in the kitchen when I came back to reality and breakfast. Instead, a note was on the kitchen table. "Don't worry about that ball" was all she had written.

"Something tells me the date didn't go too well," Maple said as she shuffled into the kitchen.

"Did you talk to her this morning?" I asked.

"Didn't have to." She started to make a smoothie.

I poured myself a bowl of Honey Nut Cheerios and checked my computer home page for the soccer scores. Madrid had won, and Meacham had scored two goals. The Red Bulls were idle. Maple sipped her smoothie and thumbed through the latest issue of *Allure,* which had a picture of Karen Wu on the cover. As we finished breakfast, we heard Sissy in the driveway. She told us Mom would be back for dinner.

Rumpy and I took off to the park to play soccer, and Maple went to the library nearby. But that afternoon, it was Mom, not Sissy, who picked us all up. She was very quiet on the ride home, but when we turned in to the driveway — where the skid marks from B. A. Boykin's Hummer were still visible — Mom turned off the car. She took a deep breath and said, "I've been suspended as the Moccasins coach by the league."

"I told you that would happen," Maple said. "It's because you're a woman."

"What a rotten day, Mom," I added, although her suspension didn't surprise me. "By that note you left this morning, we figured you may not have been treated like Cinderella at the ball last night, either."

"You're right. It was a terrible evening. He took me for a steak and a war movie. I'm thinking of going vegan after that. And I guess I should tell you the rest," Mom said before I could offer my condolences.

"What?" I asked.

"You've been traded. Uprooted like truffles," she said.

"How could I be traded? It's a kids' league."

"It all came to me last night when Rambo dropped me off. I just think we're done with Vertigo. And then this morning, I got the call saying they've suspended me as coach, and I took it as a sign."

"Which leaves us exactly where?" Maple asked.

"We are moving to New York," she said flatly, looking straight ahead.

We all sat in silence, and then Rumpy suddenly jumped out the backseat window and started twirling in a circle in the driveway, chasing her tail. We all knew this was how she showed delight, but this time she was spinning like a whirling dervish.

I started to laugh, then Mom joined in, and Maple wasn't far behind. It was infectious, and we were all laughing and whooping like hyenas at the zoo.

"The House of Wu!" is all Maple said between fits of laughter.

"The House of Wu," Mom echoed, nodding her head.

"The home of the Red Bulls!" I was jumping up and down in my seat.

The laughing fit continued until suddenly a loud thud came from behind us. We looked around to see Rumpy on her back with all four legs poking up into the air. I didn't know pigs could faint, but ours apparently had.

CHAPTER 10

Start Spreading the News

RUMPY

OINK! OINK! Start spreading the news! We were going to New York!

I guess I spun all the blood out of my head when I heard that my wish was being granted. The whole next week, the farm was a beehive. Ellie had a few more surprises up her sleeve. She had accepted a job as pastry chef at Flutbein's Hotel, one of the top restaurants in New York. The job came with a three-bedroom apartment on the hotel roof that overlooked Central Park.

Even Oliver had come through. Ellie's only concern was how to get the twins into a good school on such short notice. As it turned out, Oliver knew the headmaster at the prestigious New York Barton Academy, and he somehow got the kids enrolled. Not only was Barton a great school but it was located just a few blocks from the hotel.

The only one who seemed uninterested in the whole buzz of activity was Syrup. As long as she could drape herself around Maple's shoulders and be transported like Cleopatra, she seemed content to watch us pack.

After working all day, we would gather around the computer at night, looking at Web sites about the new school, our new home, soccer clubs, museums, and all the other fun things that you could find only in New York. Barley and Maple even looked up petting zoos and animal parks for me, and I scanned the photos, hoping to get lucky and find a picture of Lukie. That didn't happen, but at least in New York I would be a thousand miles closer to finding my brother.

THE NIGHT before we left, we invited our friends and neighbors for a picnic and a soccer game at Pancake Park. We played our last game as the moon rose over the hills of Vertigo. As the game ended, an unusually cool breeze sprang out of the north, and I began sniffing away, picking up strange scents from afar.

"You ready to start playing a little goalie in Central Park, Rumpy?" Barley asked.

I did a twirl and poked the ball with my snout in his direction. He sent a quick shot back at me, and I blocked it instantly.

"That is as happy as I think I have ever seen her," he said to Maple and his mom.

What a dear boy. He thought I was happy because I blocked his shot. He had no idea about the real source of my joy.

Now the ghosts in the trees didn't seem so threatening. The winds of change were sweeping us away from Vertigo to the island of Manhattan, where, somewhere among the millions of people and animals, my long-lost brother was waiting to be found.

That night, at Pancake Park, I could see that Barley and Maple and Ellie felt a little sad to be saying goodbye to our friends, and we all savored the memories of our time on the farm. But Ellie's sudden decision to move seemed to be the right one. The piles of boxes stacked on the front porch said it all. We were ready to go. I assumed that in the morning, the movers would come and load our belongings into a van, and we would pile into Ellie's Jeep and head north to our new home.

I assumed wrong.

CHAPTER 11

Family Week

Barley

When the Winnebago pulled into our driveway, my first horrified thought was that Coach Boykin was back and ready to take Mom to a tailgate party. I was even more stunned when Dad popped out of the driver's seat and said, "Anybody need a lift to New York City?" I didn't even know he could drive.

I have a feeling that Mom called him and told him our move to New York might be a good opportunity for him to spend time with Maple and me and help with the trip. To his credit, Dad jumped right in.

As we loaded the mobile home, I filled him in on my

soccer stories, past and present. He, of course, told me he had a big deal almost sold to the Fox Network. This was going to be his big break. At the end of our trip, he was heading back to Iceland to do research. Believe me, I had heard that one before. When Dad was in the chips, everybody took the ride, but when he was down on his luck, we didn't hear from him for months. I was glad our move and his good luck had coincided.

So, on a sunny morning in late August, McBride family history was made when the pastry chef, the commercial writer / TV producer, the future Red Bull star striker, the budding fashion diva, and their lazy cat and multitalented pig set off for the big city. Boy, did we smack of the Beverly Hillbillies going north.

We did a lot of singing as we crossed the Appalachian Mountains, and when we pulled into campgrounds and set up for soccer practice, people really stared. Dad attempted to play against Rumpy and me. It was immediately apparent that I did not get my athletic abilities from my father. This was pointed out repeatedly by Mom and Maple, who laughed and shouted taunts. However, we were all very impressed when Dad actually changed a tire on the Beltway outside Washington, D.C.

Then, in the early morning, just south of Philadelphia,

the whole thing began to sink in. Dad was driving, and I had fallen asleep in the passenger seat, but a loud air horn on an 18-wheeler woke me up. When I opened my eyes, a road sign read: NEW YORK — 94 MILES. I couldn't go back to sleep. It was nearly dawn, and my heart was racing. This was no dream. We were actually moving to *New York*.

OUR ARRIVAL in the Big Apple was delayed slightly because we had to drop off both Dad and the Winnebago in New Jersey, near Newark Airport. He had gotten us a different ride to town at the TV production company's expense.

The stretch limo waiting for us at the curb seemed as long as the soccer field back at Pancake Park. I could barely make out the driver's English. As it turned out, we needed every inch of the enormous limo to cram all our stuff in, which did not please the driver one bit. Mom, of course, questioned Dad's reasoning for such a large car, and Maple brought up the fact that it was a huge gas-guzzler and very "eco-negative."

"What do you mean by that?" Dad asked.

"It's not *green*," I told him.

Dad just laughed and took pictures. "It's the only way

to arrive in New York. But next time, honey, I promise I will find one that runs on french-fry oil."

My dad is not the most perceptive or practical person in the world, but it was a lot of fun to have him around, and he did promise to take me to the soccer play-offs when he returned. Besides, it was nice to be a family again, if only for a week in a Winnebago.

CHAPTER 12

Movin' on Up

Rumpy

I MUST SAY I was both surprised and pleased at the way my humans behaved on the trip north. They had made a fine little snuggling area behind the driver's seat, where I rode with my pigskin the entire trip. I had named the football "Lukie" for good luck, and the faux Lukie would keep me company until I found the real one in New York. I even enjoyed Oliver's company. He and Ellie seemed to get along a lot better than when they were married.

The limo ride into the city was a bit much. In the last scent-mail that I picked up before losing contact with Lukie, he told me about watching the circus come to New York and how the elephants had to be taken through the Lincoln Tunnel. Now *that* would be the way to arrive in Manhattan. Picking up New York scent-mails from Lukie back in Tennessee was nearly impossible, but now that I was here, finding him should — pardon the pun — be a breeze.

I was so happy as we crossed the George Washington Bridge in that ridiculous car. It was a beautiful day, and we all had our noses pressed against the tinted-glass windows of the limo, looking out at buildings that rose to the sky. Of course the McBride family couldn't make a subtle entrance. Let's start with the fact that the limo was so long, it took our driver three attempts before he could actually pull up in front of Flutbein's Hotel. The children rushed for the limo door, and I followed.

My first impression of our new home was this: *Slam! Boom!* Utter chaos! Mechanical noises clashed all around me, ominous vibrations rumbled under the streets, and each breath brought in dizzying amounts of information. My snout was bombarded with data on dogs, cats, local birds, and residents of the nearby zoo — plus their habits, owners, favorite routes, and recent meals. Suddenly I had access to the city's scent network with moment-to-moment bulletins on every neighborhood creature. Though some were full of juicy tidbits, none of the scent-mails mentioned Lukie.

When the doorman attempted to unload our belongings, suitcases tumbled to the pavement. Maple's duffel bag exploded right on the sidewalk, sending her clothes in all directions. The constant parade of people just walked around the mess and kept on going.

Ellie and Barley helped the disheveled Maple stuff her things back into her bag just as a uniformed waiter popped through the revolving front door of the hotel and brought Ellie a note on a silver tray. It was handwritten from Mr. Flutbein, the elderly and diminutive owner of the hotel, who was urgently requesting her help in the kitchen. On a whim, the king of Tonga had stopped in for lunch and was desperate for fresh pastries.

Being a Francophile as well as a charmer, Mr. Flutbein told Ellie that the head chef was on a hunting trip for the weekend, and he implored her to whip up some of her famous éclairs. She agreed to help, but before dashing off, she told us that the doorman would come back momentarily, and we were to strictly follow his lead. Then she put on her Southern charm and slipped several folded bills into the waiter's glove. Ellie left us at the entrance to Flutbein's four-star hotel, promising to return later.

THE TWINS AND I marveled at the sight of all the tall buildings. Frankly, I'm better with ground-level views. What's higher than Barley's shoulders tends to make me nervous. Well, the doorman was tall, like everything else here, and his name was Freddy. He wore a black suit with a monogrammed "F" on the jacket pocket, and he had a faint scent of his wife's perfume on his white gloves. He'd been waiting all morning for us to arrive, and we liked him from the start. His manners were exquisite for a human, and whatever he said, we could probably trust to be true.

Freddy was taking a break from the front door, and he escorted us to our apartment. Hovering in Maple's shadow, I closed my eyes as the elevator took off like a rocket ship, going higher and higher. When it opened on the roof, Freddy led us up a flight of stairs.

Along with four sets of keys, he gave us a box of the chocolates that hotel guests find on their pillows each night. Then he opened the door to reveal the oddest structure I had ever seen. It was a house – sitting on the roof! It looked like something out of *Alice in Wonderland*. Giant windows lined the walls, and a solid-glass second floor looked like an enormous planter. Outside, a broad ledge surrounded the apartment, sizable enough for sitting or walking, and a huge outdoor water heater took up the northern corner.

"Welcome to your new home," Freddy announced.

It was a far cry from our farm in Vertigo, and I felt bad for the kids. I gulped and waited for their reaction.

Maple just marched right in, and Barley said, "Cool!" After a quick inspection of the soft new carpets and wooden floors, Maple asked Freddy if it had once been an elaborate greenhouse. Freddy didn't know. Naturally, Barley disagreed, insisting it was a terrarium of the future, ideal for reptiles and highly evolved humans like him. To me, it was an overblown fish tank at best, and not remotely welcoming. Constant neatness would be necessary in such highly visible rooms, which I knew was going to be a huge challenge for Maple and Ellie. As usual, I would have to set the example.

CHAPTER 13

The Meat Thing

RUMPY

BACK IN Tennessee, the McBride family and I almost parted company, and I had to put my hoof down with regard to what was unreasonable for humans to eat.

It all started when a putrid, smoky smell began to choke me in my sleep. Dragging myself to the window for air, I thought at first that the house might be on fire, and I got ready to pull off a heroic pig rescue. Then I realized the smoke was the residue of that barbaric ritual humans refer to as "frying up breakfast meats."

I had no choice but to flee. Grabbing my pillow in my

snout, I kept my head below the fumes and raced for the door, sobbing all the way. It was a deal breaker – frying my cousins – and I slammed the door behind me as hard as I could.

The family caught up with me quickly and begged me to come home. Ellie immediately identified the problem, and she issued a decree: from that day forward, there would be no bacon on the breakfast table and no mention of the dreaded *B* word – Bar-B-Q.

For weeks, Ellie gathered nutritious recipes that involved no dead animals. The children devoured everything. A month later, I'm proud to say they looked better than ever, their smiles were more pleasant, and they were much more educated about the world of organic and healthy foods.

Both twins began to oppose the frivolous consumption of meat. Maple even went vegan. I'm not sure whether it was the fuss I made about the bacon or the lunches they served at the school cafeteria that influenced her decision, but I was happy to have a vegan in the house. In truth, though, with my sincere apologies to the nonflying bird population, my very favorite food is chicken fingers, but I felt safer keeping that secret to myself. I was thrilled that both Maple and Barley brought the plight of domesticated animals to the attention of their school class with posters and Web site postings. Barley won a class debate with his fervor on the subject. I have no doubt those two could change the world – or the universe, maybe, with a little help from Lukie and me. What we had started in Tennessee, we would continue up here in our glass house above Manhattan.

I knew we had our work cut out for us in New York. Let's just start with the hot-dog wagons. They are parked on every corner, and people line up to order. I don't even want to think about what is in those weenies. *Yuck.* And the Southern hospitality of Tennessee seemed to be in short supply on the streets.

As for manners, or should I say the lack of them, that was brought center stage when the movers showed up. As they transferred our belongings along the difficult route to our glass house, they grumbled and griped the whole time. Piece by piece, I snorted and showed them what furniture went where. Maybe they just weren't used to being nudged along by a couple of kids and a pig underfoot. When they finally finished, I gave them a lovely tip of four large bunches of carrots with greenery still attached.

"Welcome to New York," one of them grunted in what I took to be more of a warning than a compliment.

Just after the movers left, Ellie reappeared like a whirling tornado, spinning out of her flour-and-chocolate-stained apron and into fresh city clothes. She looked around the odd confines of her new home and said, "This will work fine." Then she quickly gathered the twins and dashed off to orientation at Barton Academy, leaving Syrup and me rump-deep in all the moving clutter.

AFTER REWARDING myself with a bunch of grapes that I eased out of one of the shopping bags on the table, I took a break and had a snooze with my Lukieball. The fish tank thing was still bothering me, but New York was becoming more manageable.

CHAPTER 14

A Poetic Pig

Barley

Dad sent me a Red Bulls jersey and again promised me a game the next time he saw me. I hoped he would come around more often now that we were in New York, but I had taken it upon myself to figure out how to get to my first Red Bulls game, whether Dad was with me or not. As soon as I had a weekend free and learned how to get around the city on the subway, I was going to head out to New Jersey to see my team. It was late in the season, and they were in the hunt for a play-off spot.

It only took a week of living in a glass house on top

of a high-rise in the middle of Manhattan to put some order into our lives. Between Mom's new job and our new school, we all hit the ground running.

At first, I really missed Pancake Park and our big house in Vertigo, but that faded quickly. New York, my birthplace, was where I belonged. And although the only barnyard animal we'd brought was Rumpy, the square footage we had to share was a lot smaller in New York. Rumpy was by far the neatest of the females, except when it came to eating. Her obsession with food was more difficult in our new home, especially for guests. Back in Vertigo, she had room to graze. Here in New York, I thought a few rules were in order, so I posted this on the refrigerator door:

Ladies, Pleeze

by Barley McBride

A spaceship occupied by pigs
Is nothing like the normal digs.
Its system must incorporate
A crazed-with-hunger vertebrate.
A thing routinely left intact
Might well become a piggy snack.

Her snout has powers unsurpassed
And never would she choose to fast.
Guests arriving at our door
Are warned to keep bags off the floor,
Since any package that arrives
Our pig could easily pulverize.
Her jaws will crush through any box
Containing candy, soap, or lox,
And purses bearing one Altoid
Most indiscreetly get destroyed.
Those kitchens where a pig patrols
Have quirky rules and complex goals.
With garbage but a tempting feast,
Trash is kept well out of reach.
The cook knows any pinch of food
Can titillate the piggy's mood.
Stems and cores, stalks and peels,
Recycle into stellar meals.
When backs are turned, she strikes in greed
And runs, achieving shocking speed.
She punctures all stray cans of beer
And licks them up with rising cheer.
The glass of wine left on the floor
She drains, then slips into a snore.

Impulses of our precious swine
Are far from easy to divine.
A handful of our frequent guests
She loves – while others she detests.
We welcome and appreciate
The few who think our pig is great.
So bright and winning from the start,
A constant hunger drives her heart –
Which makes it hard to reprimand
The pig we love, a shark of land.

CHAPTER 15

Welcome to New York

Rumpy

OKAY, OKAY, a *grain* of truth is in Barley's poem, but *pleeze!* Such exaggeration. Then again, it shows a healthy respect for my appetite. Maple calls it an unharnessed force of nature, and Barley says when there's food around, I'm a hurricane in reverse. But the twins are easily impressed.

Speaking of impressions, let's just say Barton Academy initially made a big one on both Maple and Barley. From the moment they stepped off 87th Street and into the tall brick building, they knew they were a *long* way from Vertigo. For Barley, it was the sports teams, and, of course, soccer season started the year. For Maple, it was the ripe little plum of information that Karen Wu had actually been a *student* at Barton Academy, and she was on the board of directors of the school. Maple needed no more motivation. The twins never once mentioned what must have been a huge shock — going to a city school with a cramped playground, a curious student body, teachers with foreign accents, uniform blazers, and the disruption caused by sirens, horns, and construction equipment that would be the constant background noise in their education.

Then there was the social side of things. Luckily for my twins, they were immediately perceived by the city kids as cool — not as hicks from the sticks. I must admit, I think I played a part in that, because Maple told us how fascinated the city kids were with her story about a pet pig that did a tango imitation of P. Diddy at a talent contest. Yes, I can make a curtain call when asked.

New York kids simply couldn't believe that anybody had a pig for a pet. Boy, were they in for a surprise. I felt my New York debut was just around the corner. Maple would design my costume, and I would be a hit. I heard that New York audiences were tough and much more sophisticated than what I was used to in Tennessee, but I knew I could handle them. Still, I had not come to New York just to be in the spotlight.

Once we were moved in, I had to get down to business; it was time to find Lukie. Scent-mails were in the air, but there was no sign yet of my brother. This meant I'd have to go back to basics and sniff a few streets. I wasn't going to find Lukie by blogging some MySpace site. One of the good things about living in the glass house on top of the hotel was that it took on the function of an observation post. From there, my short-legged view of the world was magnified immensely. I felt as if I had stepped into the tallest pair of elevator shoes in the world.

One day, while pondering how to find Lukie, I saw that the sky above me was suddenly darkened by a strange gray cloud. Upon closer inspection, I realized that it wasn't a cloud at all but a flock of pigeons. They swooped across my view as if they were trying to tell me something. Suddenly it dawned on me that notifying the pigeons would be an excellent tactic, since they could see everything in the city.

This uptown-downtown flock seemed to patrol the airspace above and around Central Park. Maybe — if the pigeons would cooperate with me — I could begin my search for Lukie tomorrow morning after Ellie went to work and the kids were off to school. That left the rest of the afternoon to see the city. I made my way out of the fish tank, down the service elevator, and across the alley to the street. As soon as I stepped onto the sidewalk, I was overwhelmed again.

A handsome horse smiled at me from where his carriage stood. Green grass and flowers lined the streets. The air was filled with the smell of lunchtime, which brought happy tears to my eyes . . . and a tiny trickle of drool to my lips. I was thrilled to find that there was more to this town than just hot dogs. Everywhere I went, I saw pretzels steaming, popcorn spilling, and restaurant doors wide open. With such dazzling food every few feet, no wonder people were drawn here.

I sat to observe the locals and was struck by how unlike other humans they were. Each was crisply dressed and pressed for time, and seemed to be suffering from stress. Lacking the plumpness I was used to seeing in Tennessee, the local humans were more angular. Stylish yet emaciated, the ladies shared a facial expression I knew well: the intense longing for something to eat. They were shockingly underfed, considering the abundance of food in sight.

One man, however, was trying to address the problem. He stood in the park in front of a huge blender, making fruit smoothies, which he was distributing to anyone interested – if they stood in front of the blender. Famished, I ambled over to join the line and lap one up.

To my amazement, the people nearby screamed at me in fear and backed away, nearly running. Desperate to calm them, I spotted an accordion player and instantly picked up his beat, moving my haunches to the rhythm. But this made the humans more frantic than ever, shouting, "Get back! It must be rabid!" and "Run! It's about to attack!"

Their reaction was entirely bizarre. A man poked his head out of a kebab wagon next to the smoothie stand and cursed me for running off his crowd. In a terrible rage, he began hurling soda cans at me, and others followed his lead but used rocks instead. When a sharp one hit my shoulder, I broke into a whimpering run and flew back the way I had come. Bleeding and disheartened, I skidded through the service doors and onto the freight elevator.

What was the problem? I had come to New York with open hooves to embrace the city, its people, and its animals, but everybody was treating me as if I were a terrorist. I was accustomed to good manners, admiration, and, frankly, even star treatment. Now I was finally where I wanted to be, but everything was wrong.

How did Lukie survive here, where pigs were considered monsters? By the time I got home, I was emotionally wrung out. For once, I *wasn't* hungry. All I wanted to do was get to Maple's closet, find my Lukieball, and cuddle up.

When I crept through the kitchen, I heard Barley in the living room, talking to someone. I stopped for a moment at the open door. Barley wouldn't look at me, but I knew he knew I was there. Something strange was going on, and I had seen enough strange stuff for one day. I headed for the closet. It crossed my mind that Barley might be protecting me . . . and then the truth slapped me in the face: New York was filled with prejudice, and my kind wasn't welcome.

When we had arrived that first day, and we saw the Statue of Liberty in the distance, Barley quoted the words written on the base: "Give me your tired, your poor, your huddled masses . . ."

But those words were clearly for *people,* not pigs.

CHAPTER 16

Warning Signs

BARLEY

WHEN YOU grow up with a pig as a pet, the click of tiny hooves supporting a lot of weight is an absolute giveaway of her presence. It sounds like somebody is walking around in tap shoes all the time. When I heard the *click, click, click* come from the kitchen, it wasn't the sound but the pace at which her legs were moving that clued me in that something was up. Ordinarily, I would have immediately followed and found Rumpy to make sure she was all right, but I had a bigger problem. After I came back from soccer practice, I had encountered a garrulous man with a high-pitched voice who smelled of motor oil and cigarettes. What was most disturbing about this stranger was the fact that he was in our home alone. He introduced himself as the hotel building superintendent and said he was there to check out our pipes and wall sockets, but I had a hunch he was snooping around.

The man's name was Murray, and Freddy, the doorman, had warned me about him a few days earlier. Freddy had also told me that maybe it was best not to have so many people over to see Rumpy do her thing. Then he looked frightened, scanning the lobby to see if anyone was watching us. He leaned down and, in a loud whisper, said, "Boucher, the head chef, is back in the hotel."

Murray asked way too many questions, and his eyes never met mine. His neck jerked as he went from room to room with his flashlight on and his tool belt rattling. He had gone through every room except Maple's and was heading in that direction when I said, "My sister's asleep in there. She's not feeling well."

Murray shone his flashlight into the hallway and finally looked at me. "Dis uhl only take a second," he said, and started to open the door.

"We think she has the mumps," I blurted out.

Murray let go of the doorknob and clicked his flashlight off. "Well, I'm sure tings is okeydokey in dere. Hope yaz sistah gets betta."

I walked him to the door and watched as he sauntered away across the roof. Then I rushed back to Maple's room. When I opened the door, Rumpy and Syrup were piled together in the corner of the closet, asleep.

Something wasn't right. Mom would be home any minute, and I needed to talk to her.

CHAPTER 17

Traveling at the Speed of Dreams

Rumpy

I WAS DREAMING. I was back in Vertigo, sitting at a desk. Using my hooves, I was able to type on the computer, and I could see Flutbein's Hotel on the screen. Barley and Maple were in the fish tank on top of the hotel, but in my dream, it wasn't a fish tank; it was a spaceship, and they were sending me instant messages, telling me how much they missed me, and they were wondering if I was ever coming back to New York.

I typed back to them, "Not as long as Boucher is around."

Boucher. Now there is a name that can strike fear into the heart of any pig. In French, it means "Butcher" – as in the guy who makes pork chops and hams out of you-know-what. I had overheard that he was the head chef.

Next thing I knew, I dreamed I was back in the fish tank, and Maple and Barley were all abuzz because I had returned so fast.

I like to travel at the speed of dreams.

The twins were smoothing my coat and asking me how I had learned to type so well. Barley mentioned his concern about my love of exploring. Maple seemed to feel I was searching for someone . . . and there the dream melted into cheeses dancing with tomatoes! Though I was sleeping, my very alert and sensitive snout was still on and engaged in its most frenetic twitch, announcing, like the scream of an airport metal detector, a fresh pizza – my second-favorite food next to chicken fingers. This meant Ellie had brought dinner home after a long day of work.

"Supper's here, girls," Barley announced. I was back to reality in a second. I scrambled out of the closet and raced to the living room, where the picnic of my dreams lay spread across the floor. Edible flowers had been scattered like a path to four pizzas, surrounded by freshly baked apples.

In spite of the hostility below in the mean streets, that night in the fish tank was pure heaven. Ellie raved about the hotel's modern kitchen. It was every chef's dream, and she was determined to please Mr. Flutbein with her work. She had introduced herself to the waiters and had asked them for feedback on any dessert. Over coffee, the busboys told her amusing stories about the regular guests, as well as a few good jokes. The senior chef, a Frenchman by way of Hackensack, New Jersey, had returned from his hunting trip. Ellie described the way he snarled at his employees and was constantly ducking into the alley behind the kitchen for a cigarette.

"You mean Boucher?" Maple asked. Syrup hissed from her shoulder.

"Sounds like he might be the next candidate for the famous Coach Mom's cheap-shot payback," Barley said with a smirk.

Ellie didn't see the humor in his statement. "How do you know his name?" she asked.

Barley then told her about finding Murray in the apartment, snooping, and about Freddy's warning to watch out for the head chef.

"Well, we are all new here, and we will just have to learn to get along with everybody. I assure you that the good apples here at the hotel certainly outnumber the bad ones."

Apples. *Mmmmm.* I confess I wasn't thinking about the rotten apple that had just appeared in my dreams an hour earlier. No, I was thinking more about the nicely baked ones placed around the pizzas. I didn't need an invitation. I gobbled the apples while the kids were telling Ellie about their day at school. Barley was excited he had made the varsity soccer team, and Maple announced that Barton's "pet day" was coming up next week. Normally I would have jumped at the opportunity to perform, but after my day at the park, I was relieved that Maple was going to take Syrup to class — so she could exhibit the extensive cat wardrobe she had made.

After dinner, Ellie came over and sat by me and scratched my head. "You seem tired, Rumpy," she said. She removed her apron and placed it next to my snout so I could get a whiff. Drenched with flavor, it was a delicious record of every meal she had served that day, and it sent me off to dreamland again — but that night, I slept fitfully on the couch. I guess three whole pizzas kept the snake dreams fueled.

In my next dream, Ellie was in the hotel kitchen, and I was her assistant. The kids were seated at a table in the dining room with Lukie, and he and Barley were wearing tuxedos. The kitchen had a glass wall, and everyone was staring at us. Ellie was creating a very strange dessert – a toffee tarantula, suspended in a spun-sugar cobweb, with yellow eyes that scanned back and forth for prey.

I should have taken it as a warning.

CHAPTER 18

More Soccer than a Boy Could Want

BARLEY

THINGS MOVE quickly here in New York. Back on the first day of school, I barely had time to get my locker straightened out because soccer tryouts started right after the end of class. The next day, the team list was posted on the bulletin board, and that afternoon, I had a practice uniform on. I was running plays as a member of the Barton Academy Falcons on the Great Lawn of Central Park. Being a new kid in a city school like Barton was not easy, but it certainly helped that I could kick a ball.

Let's just say that the Great Lawn of Central Park is a very different home field than Pancake Park. On any given day, more people are playing soccer than football! That is why the Great Lawn is where you will find me most of the time I am not in school.

Barton Academy is only a few blocks from the park, and we practice every afternoon and play our games there as well. Then there is the *big* difference, and it is a huge one: the Red Bulls practice at Giants Stadium, just across the Hudson River in New Jersey. I finally figured out the subway-and-bus route there, and Mom is going to take me over next weekend. The Red Bulls are tied for first place in the East with D.C. United. Who knows, I just might get to that play-off game with Dad after all.

In the meantime, our first game was simply amazing. I have to say I'll never forget running onto that field in the middle of Central Park, scoring the winning goal, and actually hearing more than four people cheer. It kind of signaled that I had really *arrived* in New York – even more than when I had tumbled out of the stretch limo. Mom and Maple were in the crowd, and all of Maple's new school friends were text-messaging her, asking if I had a girlfriend. *Yuck!*

When I am not playing for the Falcons, I can just go to

the park with my ball and find any one of a dozen pickup games on the lawn. I play with everybody, from kids my age to grown men who don't speak much English. Already my Spanish has improved tremendously. So I can honestly say that soccer is not only fun but also educational. Still, I have to leave time to do my schoolwork back in the fish tank. Soccer is sure more fun, but Barton is an academic challenge, and I promised Mom that I would make good grades in order to play soccer. It's only been a few weeks, but so far so good.

There is only one problem with having all the soccer a boy could want. Because of the almost unlimited supply of games, players, and shots on goal, my longtime goalie, Rumpy, sort of slipped off my radar and onto the sidelines. Back in Vertigo, Rumpy was always in goal, because most of the time we didn't have enough humans to make up a team. But in New York, that just wasn't the case.

After our second Falcons game, Mom pointed out that I had left Rumpy out. She was right, and I felt bad. Not only was Rumpy our pet but she was my pal — and kind of like a roommate, too. That night, I promised Mom that I would spend time with Rumpy in the park. I had just gotten distracted by all the great things to do in the city, especially in Central Park. There were concerts, bike trails, restaurants, and the zoo. There was even a castle on the Great Lawn.

Mom laughed and reminded me that she, too, had been a country girl who had come from Mississippi to the Big City. "No matter what great changes life brings you," she said, "you have to make time for your true friends, Barley." And that is exactly what I did. After practice the next day, I sprinted to the Barton bookstore and bought Rumpy a surprise. But when I got home, I found her buried in the corner of Maple's closet, hugging that football of hers.

There was no wiggle and no rush to rub my leg and get scratched. She showed no interest in my gift, and she didn't even react when I told her about our upcoming one-on-one playdate. Instead, she simply looked up at me, rolled over, and closed her eyes. Maybe she was feeling bad after eating three pizzas the night before, or maybe she was just homesick for the farm. Anyway, it was my job to cheer her up, and I was taking that job seriously.

CHAPTER 19

Not So Fast There, Rumpy

RUMPY

I GUESS I needed that fourteen-hour nap after the incident in the park and the pizza dreams. I woke up early the next morning feeling much better. I had a faint memory of Barley in the closet talking to me, but I couldn't remember what he had said. Then I saw his gift — the prettiest red jersey with FALCONS written across the front and my name and the number "1" stitched across the back. Next to it was a snout guard that Maple had designed with the Barton Academy colors. They hadn't forsaken me! I was back in the game. I was still Barley's goalie, and I was still Maple's favorite star to dress.

It was exactly the medicine I needed. Maybe New York wasn't such a bad place after all. I jumped up and began to scratch around Maple's bed, even before her alarm rang. She rolled around in the covers, but I pulled on her sheets.

Just then, Barley popped his head in the door. "There's my goalie!" he said with a smile. I ran over to him and snuggled up, grunting and spinning at his feet, stopping only long enough for Barley to get my new jersey on. Maple took a picture of me.

As usual, the kids got dressed for school, fixed their breakfast and mine, and packed up their schoolbags. Ellie's absence during this morning ritual wasn't unusual; she often dashed to the kitchen early to make sure the overnight bakers had cooked the morning pastries properly. I walked in front of the mirror in the hallway and admired my new jersey. I was ready to take on New York again.

I had often walked the kids to school in Vertigo, and I had figured it would be the same in New York. However, I opted to lie low. I was scared to go out. But the jersey cheered me up and boosted my confidence. Suddenly I was looking forward to exploring the route to Barton Academy and seeing what kind of goalie the Falcons had. Once the twins were safely in class, I could scout the streets around the campus for Lukie scents before checking out soccer practice in the park. Then I would try to connect with the uptown pigeons. My hope was that they were in contact with other pigeon squadrons in the city. Working together, they could help me locate Lukie. I was back on the job.

THAT AFTERNOON, I was chewing away on the last carrot in my bowl when the scent of fresh-baked croissants made its way into the kitchen. Ellie must have returned from the restaurant. "What?" I heard Barley yell. "That's *outrageous!*"

I stopped eating and ran for the living room.

"Oh, Rumpy . . ." Maple said in a shaky little voice.

"It's just not fair!" Barley shouted. He had tears in his eyes, and his voice was angry.

Ellie stooped down and stroked my head. "Rumpy, you can't go out anymore."

Apparently one of the waiters had been telling everyone that a pig at a hot-dog stand had been chased by a mob through the park.

"It was you, wasn't it?" Ellie asked.

The truth was written all over my face.

Ellie was crying now. "Oh, Rumpy," she said, "it's all my fault. I was too busy worrying about the move. I never imagined the problems city life would present for a pig. And then *this* showed up under our door this morning."

Barley held up a letter written on hotel stationery. He read the large print at the top:

"No Exotic Pets Allowed." He went on, "This includes ocelots, mice, chinchillas, monkeys, ferrets, gerbils, hamsters, reptiles, prairie dogs, sheep, goats, rats, and . . . pigs." Barley stopped reading. He crunched the paper into a ball and kicked it into the trash can in the corner.

"I think that's why Murray was snooping around the apartment," Ellie said. "The waiters told me he and Boucher have been lobbying Mr. Flutbein to get rid of all hotel pets except cats and dogs. Then, just yesterday, someone brought his pet ocelot into the lobby. Somehow it spotted a mouse in the corner of the dining room and got free from its owner. The ocelot bounded across five full tables of diners before it leaped onto the buffet — imagine an ocelot and a *mouse* in this hotel! Boucher went berserk. And I guess Mr. Flutbein finally agreed with him."

The room went silent.

"This is not right," Barley said.

"I'm afraid New York is not Tennessee." Ellie scratched me behind my ears. "I fear your inexperience with city life has put you at a big disadvantage here, Rumpy, and quite possibly in grave danger."

Ellie went on to explain that she had been pacing all morning, trying to figure out what to do. She had signed a contract with the hotel, we couldn't return to our old life for a year, and she really needed the money. Shipping me back to Tennessee or sending me to live in a local petting zoo was out of the question. That left only one option: confinement to quarters. She had made the decision that they would hide me until she had gotten to know her boss better. Then she could plead our case. After all, we really didn't live in the hotel but on the roof. In the meantime, I had to stay out of sight, which was a big order for a pig living in a fish tank.

Maple kissed me good-bye. Barley knelt down beside me. I couldn't look at his face, and he didn't know what to say. Biting his lip, he scratched my ears a little bit on his way out. "Don't worry, Rumpy," he said, petting me through my Falcons jersey. "You'll be back on the field in no time."

And then they were gone. Welcome to my lonely world.

CHAPTER 20

An Unwanted Exotic

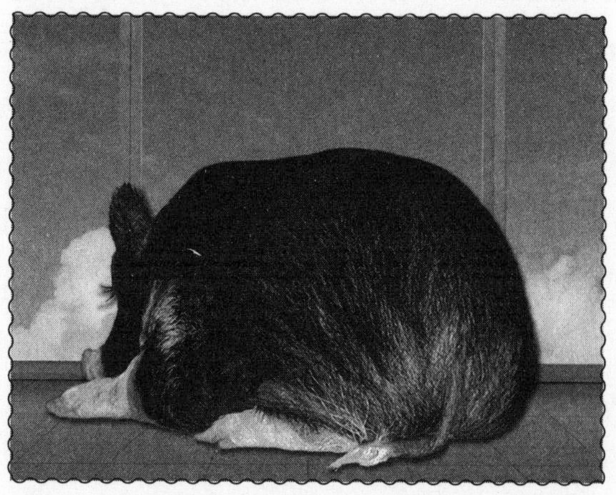

Rumpy

I WAS A PIG without playmates, a goalie without a net to guard, and an orphan on an island.

I understood that Ellie had made a very difficult decision, and in the larger picture of life on the planet, humans and animals had suffered and endured much worse hardships. Although I would now be in hiding, I was a thick-hided potbellied pig and would do whatever it took to find Lukie.

I had to think positively, so I wore the Falcons jersey and watched Barley play soccer from my "skybox." Maple even stitched button eyes, small triangular ears, a little snout, and a big smiling face on my Lukieball.

It worked for a while. At first, I rearranged my closet hideout a dozen different ways, but then I got bored. Next, I took up hunting. Well, kind of. I used my "smell-evision" to help Syrup survey the corners and crevices of the fish tank for unwanted rodents, but in a glass house, there aren't many places for even mice to hide. Syrup soon took her game outside to the rooftop, which was off-limits to me.

As the days got shorter and the weather got colder, my perch above the city turned from a skybox into a prison. For hours every day I stared out the window at the people and animals below on the street. Morning rush hour slowly transformed into evening rush hour as thousands of humans buzzed along the sidewalks. They looked like ants – so tiny and busy – holding cell phones, carrying briefcases, pushing carts . . . and even walking dogs. I desperately wanted to be in their midst, collecting information. Surely *one* of those people knew my brother.

I took to taking longer naps and put on a few extra pounds, which Ellie noticed. That is when she came up with a small, clandestine plan that made things a tiny bit more bearable. On moonless nights, Barley and Maple would be allowed to take me for rooftop walks so I could get some exercise and fresh air. I don't know who was more excited – the twins or me.

The kids saw this as a James Bond–type mission – to walk their pig in stealth and stay out of the path of the Butcher and the Handyman. It was a job any kid would have envied, and my twins did not disappoint me.

CHAPTER 21

Double-O Pig

Barley

We took Mom's orders as if they had come from the director of the CIA. Though I had never laid eyes on the menacing Boucher, I knew he was the enemy and had to be treated as such. At first, I thought I would be more into the job than my sister, but if I was James Bond protecting our pig, Maple became the Terminator. She obsessed over every detail, including her creation of an all-black spandex spy outfit to completely disguise our pig.

From the get-go, I could see a huge change in Rumpy's

attitude. She pranced around in the dark while Maple and I alternated between lookout and trainer. Even Syrup seemed to sense her call to duty and stationed herself on the ledge, focused on the stairwell. Rumpy walked and sniffed the air intensely, as if she were tracking something or somebody. I was so happy that Rumpy was cheerful again, but it didn't take long before trouble showed up.

We were playing keep-away with Rumpy's pet football under the stars on a gorgeous night when Syrup let out a high-pitched screech from her lookout position. Suddenly we heard heavy footsteps coming up the stairs.

Maple had anticipated such a moment, and she had cleverly arranged some giant planters and empty crates into a kind of hidden bunker. As we scurried into the shelter, the rooftop door was flung open, and a tall, skinny man in a long coat stomped toward the glass house and began banging on the door. A lit cigarette glowed in the corner of his mouth.

"Ellie! Ellie!" he shouted.

As we stared at the man through a narrow crack, we didn't have to ask who it was. It was Boucher.

A waiter followed him, dressed in a tuxedo.

Again, Boucher banged on the door. "Where is that idiot woman?" he sniped. "I knew I would catch her sneaking away from work to bring dessert to her despicable little brats." He banged again on the door, yelling Ellie's name as he tossed the lit cigarette over the ledge and immediately lit another one. Even hidden in our bunker on the other side of the roof, we could smell his trail of Turkish smoke, garlic, and wine.

Just then, the waiter's cell phone rang. He answered it. "Monsieur Boucher, it is Ellie. She is waiting for you in your office."

Boucher spun on his heels and stomped back down the stairs. Silently we tiptoed out of our bunker and rushed Rumpy back into the fish tank.

We had met the enemy.

CHAPTER 22

My Four-Star Prison

RUMPY

THE ROOFTOP walks were a godsend, and my security team was better than the Secret Service. My "strolls around the prison yard" gave me access to the open air and to scents — but twenty-five stories up, the signals were faint. Still, I sniffed for Lukie, but there was not much written on the wind. Oh, to be a pig with wings.

During the day, I watched the trendy fashions on the people below. I couldn't believe how many of them always wore black, as if they were dressed for a funeral. And then there were all the slovenly dogs who pranced about freely. They insulted my shriveled pride – all immodestly scratching themselves and spreading their fleas. Marking their territory like some kind of canine conquerors, they lifted their legs on anything they passed.

Just as I was starting to feel more like a city pet than a Tennessee tango dancer, fall gave us a tease of winter. One morning, the chubby weatherman on TV – who I considered a friend – did a fake shiver as he announced the sudden arrival of an arctic cold front. Blustery winds roared in from Canada, blowing the leaves off the trees and sending Manhattan residents scurrying for cover. It rattled the glass fish tank, and everything from newspapers to flying squirrels blew by the windows.

The kids happily donned their winter coats, scarves, mittens, and earmuffs. I could barely see their eyes when they told me good-bye. Staring out the window that morning, I worried that the approaching winter might seriously limit the little freedom I now possessed.

ELLIE AND MAPLE had just walked in when the phone rang.

"Someone is coming up to see us. Hide that pig!" Ellie said to Maple. The call must have come from Freddy, because he announced all visitors to the fish tank except the sneaky ones who worked in the kitchen.

I was bolting for the closet when the apartment buzzer rang. “What in the name of heaven?” I heard Ellie blurt out, but laughter followed.

My curiosity got the best of me, and I looked at the door. There stood a man wearing a complete Red Bulls home uniform. For a moment I thought it might be Oliver, up to one of his elaborately planned unannounced visits, but the person was much too short.

“Barley, what are you doing in that outfit?” Maple asked. “Those pants need to be taken up.”

“It’s a present from Dad, but I have even bigger news,” Barley said, all excited. “I’ve been invited to try out for the Red Bulls Youth Academy.”

I followed Maple to the computer, where she was already Googling. Barley pointed to an article. “Look, it says here that the Red Bulls set the pace in Major League Soccer as the only professional team to boast a regional development school. I was just invited to try out for it, as soon as our season’s over. A scout for the Red Bulls has been coming to our games. Today, after practice, Coach told me about it.”

Barley looked so happy. I tried to act cheerful, but I

knew what was happening. The kids were beginning to love the joys of city living more than they loved me. The twins now adored the strange glass house, and Ellie had become an overnight success with her pastries. Filled with pride, Mr. Flutbein dined in the restaurant every night. Midmeal, he'd stand, tap his cane to hush the room, and call Ellie out to take a bow. The room would burst into applause, much to the chagrin of Monsieur Boucher. However, Boucher did acknowledge her talent — by using it to his advantage. For Mr. Flutbein's birthday party, he assigned Ellie the preparation of two hundred pastries and a seven-tiered D'Auberge cake with an ice-cream core. At the last minute, of course, Boucher would take all the credit.

However, our Ellie got one in on the Butcher. Despite his orders, she made something else. As Boucher was describing his creation to Mr. Flutbein, Ellie unveiled a completely different dessert. It was a collection of erupting volcanoes, sitting on small edible maps. Each volcano spewed out chocolate lava, which filled the seas and then covered the nearby Isles of Meringue. It made the cover of *New York* magazine, and sweet-toothed cartographers flew in from all over the world and waited in line for hours to eat at Flutbein's and watch their volcanoes blow.

At first, the Butcher was furious, but when the long lines began to form in front of the restaurant, he simply took credit for the success.

As for Ellie, fame can produce a caravan of the curious, especially if you live in Manhattan. First there were the suitors. Any single woman who cooked and looked like Ellie did was bound to draw the attention of men on the prowl for that perfect girl. A constant parade of them made reservations at the restaurant just to eat Ellie's desserts and send requests to meet the dessert chef. A few of them actually came to the door of the fish tank when Ellie was home, clutching bunches of flowers and boxes of chocolates. None of them was as bad as Coach Boykin, but none of them gained the approval of the panel of judges seated on the couch.

Ellie always looked fabulous on her dates. She spent so much time in Flutbein's kitchen, wrapped in a baker's apron, that when she went out, she dressed to the nines. But as stunning and talented as Ellie was, her suitors always had the same reaction when they were introduced to us. The excitement in their hopeful eyes switched instantly to confusion when they met the twins and watched me snort and wave a leg from my perch on the couch.

A pig and two kids aren't much baggage, if you ask

me. But the guys always blurted out the same question: "Gee, how old is that thing?"

"*She*," Ellie would reply.

"How old is *she*?" they would repeat.

Ellie always laughed, scratched my head, and said in a coy voice, "You never ask a lady her age."

Like clockwork, that prompted the follow-up: "Well, uhhh, how long do they tend to live . . . ?"

Ellie usually let that one hang in the air as she took the candy and flowers from the man's hand and set them on the table, to be replaced by her arm. Out she would go, into the night. Then the kids would attack the sweets and toss me the flowers to munch. We ate with confidence, knowing that Ellie would have a fun evening but be returned to us by midnight.

We knew we were big obstacles to any serious romance — but we were selfish in that regard. We wanted Ellie all to ourselves, and the odds were that two kids, a lovely pig, and a job that woke her at five every morning would keep her in our lives for quite a while.

CHAPTER 23

Road Trip

BARLEY

SOCCER SEASON seemed to fly by like a speeding subway train. Indian summer returned, and it was a joy playing in the cool, crisp afternoon air. I am proud to say that the Barton Academy Falcons won the division championship and the City of New York championship. We also qualified for the state championship game in Albany. More important, the Red Bulls would be announcing the statewide selections of players for their development league right after the tournament. This was a big deal. However, the state championship game was taking place on the same weekend that Mom and Maple were flying to Florida. Mr. Flutbein was going to a hotel convention in Palm Beach, and he wanted to take Mom with him to show off her volcano cake.

This, of course, did not sit well with the disgruntled Boucher, but Mom was past being intimidated by the "Hunchback from Hackensack," as the McBride family called him. Mom and Maple were very excited to go to Palm Beach, but they felt bad about missing my big game. Then there was the question of what to do with our pig. That problem was solved by – who else? – my mom.

One night I overheard her talking to my dad on the phone. She was telling him about my game. So when he called the next day and told me he was coming to New York, I acted surprised.

"Wow, your season went fast. How did I miss it?" he asked.

I didn't answer.

His voice was filled with excitement as he told me about his new job in Iceland, this time producing a TV pilot for yet another reality show. The episode was called "A Long Way from Home." He had written an article for *Pilots* magazine about a couple of cod fishermen from Iceland who had gotten blown off course and wound up in an unknown bay, where they discovered an airplane wing sticking out of the ice. It turned out that the wing belonged to one of six planes that had been lost in a storm back in World War II. Dad's story had been read by the son of one of the original pilots, and now the son owned an airline. He financed an expedition to find the planes and paid for Dad to go along and write about it.

When the expedition found the planes, the producers at Fox wanted Dad to alter the real story and make up an idiotic version that claimed the planes were wreckage from an alien invasion.

"If people believe the *X-Files* are real, I guess they'll buy anything. Besides, it's a paycheck," Dad said.

We finally got to talk about the state championship, and he sprung his "surprise" on me: he was coming to town and taking me to the game. He also mentioned that since the Red Bulls were in first place, he was working on our play-off tickets. I didn't let myself get too excited about that. I just checked my watch and figured it was way past midnight in Iceland. Mom had always told me to never count on anything my dad said after midnight. Anyway, I didn't really care about the Red Bulls tickets at that moment. I was just happy my dad was coming to New York.

So Maple and my mom packed their summer clothes

like sorority sisters heading for spring break. Mom ran down to the hotel kitchen to tie up a few loose ends, and Rumpy nudged their suitcases to the door and gave us a sad look.

"Rumpy," Maple told her, "I have a surprise for you, but you have to keep it a secret from Mom."

For weeks, Maple and I had been trying to think of a way to sneak Rumpy out of the hotel without anybody seeing her. It would be great for her to get some exercise and fresh air.

"Let me show you something I've been working on," Maple continued. Then she took Rumpy behind the black curtain that hid her sewing machine. After a few minutes of wiggling and giggling and snorting, Maple came back out, followed by a . . . *sheepdog!*

"Ta-da," she said, beaming.

Well, I almost couldn't believe it. The pet ban at the hotel applied only to exotic animals. Maple had made a custom sheepdog costume for Rumpy that fit her like a glove. "It's not quite finished," Maple said. "It was supposed to be for Halloween, but I think it will work for the trip to Albany."

To say our pig was happy would be a huge understatement.

"I think this costume might make it a little easier to sneak you out of the hotel," Maple told Rumpy, "but I'm not sure Mom would approve. So let's just keep this to ourselves." Maple hid the costume just as Mom was walking in the door.

I told Rumpy to stay in the closet. I would be right back after I took a taxi with Mom and Maple to the airport and met Dad there when he arrived. The McBrides were stepping out.

Mom and Maple's plane for Florida left before Dad's plane arrived, so I saw them off and headed over to his airline. I was excited. The Falcons were going on the road. It was the first time I had ever been to an away game with my dad, and this wasn't another scorching-hot afternoon in Huntsville. We were going to the New York State championships in Albany. And I would have my favorite goalie along for practice – provided Maple's disguise worked.

Dad bounded off the plane in Bermuda shorts and a Windbreaker, odd clothing for someone coming from Iceland, but that's my father. There was no stretch limo this time to take us to town. Instead, we grabbed a cab and headed to the hotel to pick up Rumpy.

On the way to the city, I filled Dad in on life in the fish

tank and the situation with Rumpy and Boucher. He, of course, claimed that if he saw this guy, he would punch him in the nose.

"That might not be a very good idea, Dad, unless you've won the lottery and can buy Mom her own restaurant."

Dad dropped the idle threat, and the subject switched to soccer. The traffic moved at a snail's pace, and I took full advantage to take my dad through the entire season, play by play. As I finished the details of the last game, we were crossing the bridge into Manhattan. Dad opened the window and started making trumpet sounds in the back of the cab. Then he switched into his sports-announcer voice.

"Ladies and gentlemen — senors and senoritas *et* Red Bulls fans *de todo el mundo!*" People in the cars around us began staring at him. Heads were turning in our direction. Even our cabdriver glanced in the rearview mirror. I slid down in my seat, partly embarrassed but also laughing at my crazy father. He wasn't finished.

"That's right! Right here in this taxi is the star striker for the Barton Academy Falcons. He is heading to do battle in Albany for the state championship." Now it was just embarrassing, but Dad wasn't through. "He takes with him on this journey a good-luck charm from his teammates in Madrid – *buennnnno sueerrrte,* Barley McBride!" Then, out of his bag, he produced a beautiful soccer ball.

I knew instantly that it was a Real Madrid ball. I could smell the newness. Dad held it out, and just as I was about to take it and thank him, he spun the ball in his hands. There, written across it, were the words "Barley, *Bueno Suerte!* – Darryl Meacham." I didn't know how my dad had done it, but he had gotten a ball autographed by my hero. I couldn't believe it.

By the time we arrived back at the hotel, I had thanked him, hugged him, and kissed him countless times. We rushed in. Up in the fish tank, Rumpy had heard us coming and was standing at the front door, wagging her tail.

Let's just say that Dad and Rumpy had not developed the same kind of family affection that the rest of us enjoyed. Still, she seemed happy to see him.

"Maple really outdid herself," Dad said when he saw Rumpy's costume. He promised to keep it a secret. "You would never guess that she is a pig in sheepdog's clothing." He laughed and laughed at the whole thing.

"Rumpy, Dad and I are taking you with us," I said. She always seemed to understand what I was saying and began doing her twirling thing. "So what exactly do we do with her?"

Dad simply said, "Barley, I am in show business. All

we do is dress her in that dog suit and walk out of here like we own the joint. Nobody will dare bother us. You get her ready to roll. I'll go to Hertz and pick up the van. See you in thirty."

Getting Rumpy ready meant filling a cooler with enough food to keep her happy, and I was already packed. She hadn't been out of the building since the beginning of my soccer season, and here it was, the *end* of my soccer season. I was happy she was going to be able to run around – and more important, she would see my game.

Thirty minutes later, Dad was back, and we led Rumpy to the mirror before we left. She stood there for a few seconds and then started snorting and spinning.

"It seems the girl likes her outfit," Dad said as he rubbed the top of my head. "It's showtime!" he added, clapping his hands. "Watch out, Albany! We have a championship to win!"

CHAPTER 24

No Whining

RUMPY

BARLEY'S NOT lying. This pig has never been an Oliver McBride fan. I always thought he spent more time promoting himself than taking care of his family. But when he walked me through the revolving door of Flutbein's Hotel and back into the real world, I decided to cut him some slack — for now. I was a free pig, if only for a day. It didn't even matter that the Butcher shared the revolving door with us, although I knew he would be asking Murray about the new dog in the hotel. Once inside the van, Barley unzipped my disguise and put me in the backseat so I could see out. Fall was in the air as we crossed the Tappan Zee and drove along the Hudson River toward the capital of New York State.

I had almost forgotten about Halloween, but it wasn't my costume that reminded me of the upcoming holiday. It was all those bright-orange pumpkins for sale on the side of the road. Though we were in a hurry to get to the game, Barley got Oliver to stop at a roadside stand to buy me one. There is nothing that tastes as good as a freshly picked ten-pound pumpkin. I ate every shred of it, even the stem.

Barley, of course, had mastered the controls of the onboard GPS unit. We drove for a few more hours, and then Barley got us right to the stadium. He zipped me into my costume, and I shot like a rocket out of the van and onto the playing field. Barley strapped on my snout guard, and I fielded his shots for an hour before the team bus showed up. I overcame my disgust over the hot-dog smoke that filled the air from countless grills at tailgate parties in the parking lot. Nothing was going to spoil these precious moments with my boy.

Before we knew it, the game was on. Barley was amazing, leading his team down the field, shouting out directions, and always keeping the ball moving. He scored an incredible goal with a header to the corner of the net at the end of the first half, but I am sad to report that it was the only goal the Falcons could muster that day. They were outgunned by an extraordinary team from Binghamton.

Losing is not an easy thing in the human world of sports competition, but I was so proud of the way Barley handled it. He didn't whine or make excuses. He just said the other team had more opportunities to win. During the drive home, he fell asleep on the backseat, and I stayed up front with Oliver, relaxing on top of my costume.

The darkness that accompanies the changing season seemed to come more quickly than usual that afternoon. I knew it was back to the fish tank and my four-star prison. I admit that during the Falcons game there were a few times when I had the urge to make a dash for the woods. But the thought quickly faded; I knew that running away was selfish and would never be the path to finding my brother. Instead, I turned my attention back to the game and snorted and twirled for my boy on the field. Whether I liked it or not, I knew for some strange reason that the path to Lukie began in the fish tank.

A few blocks from Flutbein's, Oliver woke Barley up,

and he zipped me back into my outfit. The lobby was empty, and we made it to the roof without running into the Butcher, or anyone else for that matter. Oliver tucked Barley in and got me out of my dog suit. I grabbed my Lukieball, followed him into the living room, and lay down next to him on the couch.

I think Oliver liked the idea that I chose to sleep next to him, and even though I was back in the confines of the fish tank, I was feeling better about life in general. That night I dreamed that Lukie and I were playing hide-and-seek in a large field of pumpkins. He was out there, and I was going to find him.

CHAPTER 25

The Table Begins to Turn — What New Dog?

Rumpy

I DON'T KNOW how it is for humans, but in the animal kingdom, some things happen at the right time for the right reason. The tables began to turn with that trip to Albany, but it was the night after Maple and Ellie returned from Florida that my world changed dramatically.

Oliver delayed his departure back to Iceland for a day so he could see Maple, and we had a great dinner. Maple, Oliver, and Barley cooked for Ellie. They hadn't grown up around a chef without taking a few notes. Oliver and Barley made the pasta, and Maple took care of the salad. Then came my treat. The girls had brought a big box of tropical fruit back from their trip, and Maple made me a fruit salad filled with mangoes, papayas, coconut, bananas, oranges, and grapefruit. Though she tried, we would not let Ellie in the kitchen. I took up my position as goalkeeper, and she finally gave up and sat with me on the couch. It was a delicious meal.

After dinner, Ellie went with Oliver to return his van, and then he would catch a cab to the airport. The kids walked with me on the outside roof for our usual clandestine stroll, and they set up the now-routine watch for Murray and the dreaded head chef. It was Maple's night to join Syrup and stand lookout by the door. Barley and I made the big circle, as we had done a hundred times before, but for the first time in a while, I brought my Lukieball along.

I had been sheltering my most cherished possession and pampering it in its resting place as if it were a newborn, but after my trip to Albany, I had a revelation. It was not my real brother. Pure and simple, it was a football, and it was not made of pigskin. It was made of leather, and I needed to treat it more like a ball. It had nothing to do with finding my brother.

Barley tossed the football gently in my direction, and

I reacted as any good goalie would. I whacked it back toward him with my snout at twice the speed.

Barley returned the kick, and I happily chased the ball and repeated the process. Soon we found ourselves locked in a pitch-and-toss routine worse than that of any Labrador retriever I'd seen in Central Park. We were just about to wrap up our game when Maple signaled that someone was coming up the stairs. I gave the Lukieball one last slap, and I knew when it left the end of my nose that it was too much.

The ball sailed toward the edge of the building, and Barley made a mighty leap – but over the side it went.

Before I knew it, I had pawed my way up on a heating unit and was suddenly perched on the ledge.

"Rumpy, don't move!" Maple shouted out.

I wasn't about to. Barley was at the ledge in seconds and slowly directed my hooves in reverse and lowered me off. I was too shaken to even look over the ledge, but Barley and Maple surveyed the park.

"I know it's right past that park bench over there," Barley said, "but it bounced into that hedge. I can't see it."

"You run to the park and find it. I'll take care of Rumpy," Maple ordered.

Barley made a dash for the door, and Maple and I

headed to the bunker in the corner as Murray came up to check on the boiler. Fortunately he didn't stay long, and when Barley returned ten minutes later, he had a somber look on his face. "I couldn't find it," he said, "and Mom would kill me if she knew I was in the park this late, especially alone."

I got all worked up, snorting and running around in little circles. I trotted back and forth to the ledge.

"I know you can smell it, Rumpy, but how do we get you there?"

"Room service, anyone?" Maple asked with a sly smile.

"What are you talking about?" Barley said with that judgmental expression of his.

Maple just stroked the cat, which had assumed its usual position on her shoulders. "Follow me," she said.

Well, Maple led us out of the fish tank, whispering that she had been hatching my escape plan ever since the exotic-pets rule was put into place. She had clearly scouted the old rickety fire escape that clung to the back of the hotel, and we descended behind her.

The fire escape was about as scary as my few minutes on the rooftop ledge, but with one kid in front of me and the other behind, I knew I was in safe hands. Where the fire escape ended, a doorway opened to a long, narrow hallway. That led into a deserted old banquet room, where dozens of tables and chairs were stacked to the ceiling.

"I had planned on making this a surprise some night when Mom had extra work, but I guess finding your pet football is important enough for us to try it out now."

I had no idea what she was talking about, but I knew that little girl had not only seen my anguish but felt it from day one. Maple produced a small flashlight from the pocket of her jeans. "Wait here," she said. She quietly followed the beam to the far corner of the room. A minute later, Maple rolled out a room-service table covered with a long, white oversize tablecloth, which hung down to the floor. "Your chariot, Mademoiselle," she said with a thick French accent. "I have modified it a bit," she added. Then she pulled back one side of the tablecloth to reveal a large metal door, which she opened.

Let's just say that most pigs have an inherent dislike of ovens — as one might expect. Add that I had originally been brought up as a barnyard animal, and as a runt, I had been slept on, walked over, and pushed around most of my infant life. Under normal circumstances, my claustrophobia wouldn't have allowed me to come close to entering the small door of the tin box sitting in a room-service table, but these were not ordinary times. I stepped cautiously to the door and snorted as Maple gently gave my hindquarters a nudge. She continued to shine the flashlight on the open door.

Honey, not only could this child sew but she was a car builder for confined pigs. What a contraption she had fabricated! I could see that she had cut four holes in the bottom of the box for my feet.

"Okay, let's try it," Maple said. She closed the door and lowered the tablecloth. My legs fit perfectly through the holes, and a tiny window on the back side of the box gave me a view directly ahead. I felt like one of those astronauts you see on TV, climbing into a space capsule.

I looked out the little window, and Maple and Barley's heads popped into view a few feet in front of me. "Bridge to engine room," Barley said with a giggle, "engines ahead one-third."

Well, my rocket ship had no wings or boosters strapped to it, but it was my ticket out of the hotel. I walked forward, and the table above me moved, too. "Amazing," I heard the usually reserved Barley utter. "You can't see a thing. It looks just like a table."

It took us only a few more minutes to work up the routine that would get me out of the hotel and back into the park. Maple arranged the tablecloth so it didn't block my viewing window. "I've got an idea," I heard Barley say, and I saw him disappear through the door at the entrance to the banquet room. As Maple oiled the wheels with a spray can of WD-40, Barley returned, balancing a small pile of dinner dishes in his arms. He dropped them on the table with a clunk. I smelled food instantly, a leftover salad — there were definitely carrots in it and maybe some raisins and goat cheese — but as my stomach growled, my brain took over. This was not the time to be thinking about eating.

"Now it really looks like a room-service table," Barley said.

"Try it again, Rumpy," Maple said.

I moved forward, and the dishes rattled above my head.

"Perfect," she added. Maple then gave Barley the plan. She had worked out the escape route and had gone over it many times. She would lead the way, and Barley would cover the rear. If the hallway was empty, I was to just waddle along. If someone came down the hall, Maple would whistle once, and I would pull over next to the wall and stop. Room-service trays with dirty dishes piled high were a common sight in any hotel.

Our route would take us down the hall to the elevator, which we would ride to the basement. Then we would go through the door that led to the alley behind the hotel.

The pig table worked like a charm. We made the hallway without seeing a soul, and I rolled onto the service elevator with my heart pounding. Two floors down, the elevator door opened, and three maids got on. They were busy chattering away in Chinese and didn't even notice the table in the corner. I watched the elevator button light up as the floors flew by. The maids got off at four, and nobody got on.

Then, as the number-three button lit up, I smelled cigarette smoke. When the door opened, I thought I was going to have a heart attack right there in that little box. The Butcher stepped on the elevator. But it got worse. Ellie was right behind him.

I was starting to feel like a baked ham.

"Well, hello," she said with a surprised look.

Boucher was his usual dismissive self.

"Monsieur Boucher, I would like you to meet my children. This is Barley, and that is Maple."

The kids were silent. When I had watched him in the shadows of the roof and had passed him in the revolving door, I had felt his cold heart more than I had really seen him. Now, close up, he was more menacing than ever. His face was covered with acne scars, and his jawbone jutted out like a barracuda's. His long black coat was drenched with the smell of garlic and tobacco, and he was smoking on the elevator.

"Say hello, children," Ellie urged.

The kids said hello politely to Boucher the way twins do – at the same time.

"Barley and Maple? What kind of freakish names are those? And what are you grommets doing down here, anyway?"

Ellie looked shocked at Boucher's sharp words, and I guess I expected the kids to share the same panic I was feeling – but boy, was I wrong. Maple answered calmly, "Our cat got out, and one of the housekeepers told us she saw her in the laundry room."

"Maybe she fell into a stew pot or was chased by that new dog of yours," Boucher snapped, and then laughed at his own sick joke. "What idiot left this table in the elevator?"

I could see his beady eyes looking my way, and I prayed to the pig gods that he didn't see a pair of eyes looking back at him.

"I don't believe you are supposed to be smoking in an elevator," I heard Barley say from behind the table.

Boucher immediately took his eyes off the table and shot a menacing glance back at Barley. Ellie's mouth was still open, but the distraction worked. Boucher smashed the butt of his cigarette into the salad above my head. The door opened, and the bell rang.

Boucher slid off the elevator quickly. Ellie stood in the doorway for a moment and then looked back at the twins. In a loud whisper she said, "Find that cat, and get your homework done." Then she added, "What new dog?"

Ellie rushed to catch up with the Butcher, and the elevator door closed behind them. We were in the clear.

The rest of the plan worked like a charm. At the street entrance, Maple took her backpack off. Syrup climbed out of the bag, and then Maple reached in and pulled out two sweatshirts. "I had these made at the photocopy place," Maple told Barley. Stenciled on the front of the shirts were the words ASPCA RECOVERY TEAM.

Maple brought out my sheepdog suit, and they helped me into it. The twins slipped on the sweatshirts, and then they attached me to a leash. Off we went. We all looked very official, although several passing dogs gave us very strange looks.

I don't think I would have won Best in Show at the Madison Square Garden dog show, but it did get me across Fifth Avenue and into the park. I picked up the scent of my Lukieball instantly. Barley followed my lead and found it sitting against a chestnut tree.

If I could find my Lukieball, my chances of finding the real Lukie were beginning to look up.

CHAPTER 26

That's What Moms Are For

BARLEY

DAD HEADED back to his aliens in Iceland. Hopefully he'd find his pot of gold at the end of an arctic rainbow, but either way, he left behind some happy memories. After losing the state championship, the Barton Academy Falcons hung up their soccer cleats until the spring season — all but me. I did get selected to attend the Red Bulls Academy, and it was so cool.

The field was under a giant bubble dome right next

to Giants Stadium, and we played every weekend when the Red Bulls weren't in town. Soccer was now a cold-weather sport. Who would have guessed that?

The other big discovery in New York life was ice-skating. I had thought about going out for the hockey team before Red Bulls soccer had come my way, and I kind of got hooked on skating—another wonder of living across the street from Central Park, where there were huge frozen ponds when it got cold enough.

Back in Vertigo, ice was something we put in our tea every day, and snow might have fallen in Nashville three or four times in my whole life. Winter there was just a constant procession of gray clouds and cold temperatures that put people into a hibernation frame of mind. But in New York, like everything else, they made the most out of cold weather.

Maple and I attempted ice-skating for the first time one Sunday afternoon in late October, when Mom had the day off and took us to the ice rink in the park. She had brought along one of her hotel sous-chefs, a woman named Ilga who came from Finland—where ice skates must be as natural to feet as toenails. To all our surprise, we were up and gliding around in about fifteen minutes. An hour later, we had advanced beyond basic gliding and had moved on to stopping backward and crosscutting.

Maple really took to the ice like a fish to water, and as much as I laughed and fell and motored around, most of all, I enjoyed watching Maple. For a girl who had never set foot on a frozen pond, she was remarkable. And then there was the stunning blue skating outfit she had pulled together overnight. People on the ice asked her where she bought it. She beamed and answered, "I made it."

Ilga said Maple was a natural on the ice. Several of my sister's friends from school showed up at the rink, and I guess the competitive gene kicked in. By the end of the day, Maple had done her first spin. It was simply great fun, and Mom even included Rumpy. She had bought a telescope for the fish tank and had aimed it at the rink. It stood in front of our big window, facing the park, and Mom had taught Rumpy how to look through it. I know our pig is capable of things way beyond most people's understanding, but seeing her peering into a telescope atop a New York high-rise was a startling thing. Before leaving the rink, we all skated to the middle of the ice, made a circle, and waved in the direction of the fish tank on top of Flutbein's. I knew that somewhere up on the rooftops, a pig tail was wiggling.

Meanwhile, back in the soap-opera world of the hotel kitchen, all the attention Mom was receiving from food critics and diners was not going unnoticed by the

Hunchback from Hackensack. Freddy had told us the word around the hotel was that Boucher was having an ego meltdown. Maple said there is nothing in the world like a jealous male. In Mom's case, this jealousy was translated into needless tasks and constant spying. The only thing that seemed to make Boucher the least bit happy was when celebrities came to the restaurant.

We had our own name for Boucher in our house, but Freddy told us the hotel staff had nicknamed him "BCG," which stood for "Big Carnivorous Groupie." This referred to his creepy obsession with rare meat and the stars that consumed it. One of Freddy's stories was about a vegan soprano from the opera who had used her jacket to lay a chunk of prime rib to rest and had lectured the Hunchback about his entrée, stating that it still had a beating heart. Boucher, of course, showed little concern. He dismissed the opera star as a "tree-hugging animal lover," but for every vegan opera star, he had scores of famous people who loved the rare-meat buffets that oozed buckets of juicy blood. And he fawned shamelessly over each flesh-eating, chain-smoking celebrity. In framed photos lining his office wall, Boucher stood beaming alongside countless stars — as if they were his best friends.

The other rumor Freddy told us was even darker. One of the waiters said that the reason Boucher loved the historic kitchen so much was that it had once been a dungeon. He put five-foot ovens in the old stone wall, and in the corner, where he hung a velvet curtain, an icy draft filtered over the floor. The midnight mop girls refused to cross the room, swearing his corner was haunted. Sorrowful stories circulated of a padlocked freezer room with animal bodies hanging from above in ten-degree temperatures. One of the mop girls told the others what she'd seen through the keyhole: the haunches of an elephant, a dozen frozen koalas, two pandas already sectioned, and a frozen net filled with baby dolphins.

When we told these stories to Mom, she said Boucher was not a day at the beach, but she dismissed the lurid tales as gossip. I wanted to get even, but Mom told me that was the wrong approach. She needed the job, and things would work out in the end. She assured us that karma eventually takes care of people like Boucher, and that nothing he did would cause her to rip off her apron and quit. She told us that soon she would speak to Mr. Flutbein about the exotic-pet ban — after she had gotten to his heart. She would do this as any great chef would: through his stomach. In the meantime, she reminded us that our responsibility was to keep Rumpy out of the sight of the paparazzi-pandering Frenchman.

I guess that's what moms are for.

CHAPTER 27

A Pig in Sheepdog's Clothing

Rumpy

Well, I was a pig in sheepdog's clothing after the rescue of my Lukieball. Even though I was back on the roof, I now had my telescope.

What a wonderful gift Ellie had given me! Sure, I could watch the kids ice-skate, but I could also use the scope to scan the skies. I wasn't looking for ordinary pigeons that dive-bomb the sidewalks for food. I was looking for that special squadron I had seen flying high as if they were on patrol. So far I didn't seem to be on their radar, but sooner or later they had to spot me.

It didn't take long. One day they came speeding down Fifth Avenue just above the trees, and then they made a precision turn over the zoo. They landed together on one of the big rocks by the road.

I kept my eye glued to them. They seemed to be taking a break. I had to get down there, and now I had the means to do it.

The kids were off at school, and Ellie was down in the hotel kitchen. She wouldn't be back until around five. Superman may have had his phone booth, but Superpig had Maple's closet. I coaxed the sheepdog outfit off its hanger and onto the floor, where I stuffed myself into it in record time. Once I was camouflaged, I headed for my traveling machine hidden in the deserted banquet room. I knew I wasn't supposed to use it unless the kids were around, but this was an emergency. I had to get to those pigeons.

I loaded myself like a torpedo into a tube, and I made my way out of the hotel. I overcame my urge to speed down the hallway like a skateboarder and took my time getting down the elevator. I came out the side entrance, where the flower trucks made their deliveries.

I left my table on the loading dock, and as much as it went against my grain as a pig, I tried to act like the dogs I had seen. I even raised my leg at the first tree I passed on my way into the park.

I had to find the pigeons. My vision was a little blocked by the costume, but I finally spotted the rock in the distance. I hurried toward it, only to arrive just as the pigeons lifted off in formation. I watched them circle and dive, and then they turned toward downtown. Of course I was disappointed, but I wasn't discouraged. I had made my way out of the four-star prison by myself. I was on my way to freedom.

My second escape from the fish tank came off again without incident. I pretended to be sleeping late while the kids and Ellie went through their morning routine for work and school, but once they were gone, so was I. I memorized the direction of the day's breeze, along with the dominant smells.

I did not see the pigeons that day, but I made a very important discovery — a subway map of New York and the surrounding boroughs. A gift from the pig gods! I memorized it before I gobbled it up. Now that I could combine smells with locations, New York didn't seem so daunting.

The following day, I was at it again. This time, there was less airborne clutter, and I could finally start using that God-given snout of mine. The wind was coming from the river, and it was alive with information. You name it, it was in the air: smells from Mexican kitchens, Korean grocery stores, Laundromats, fish markets, and flower shops. Often I picked up chatter from residential pets . . . but only cats or dogs, never pigs.

I spotted the pigeons once again, but they were very high up and moving fast. On the ground, bakery exhaust fans perfumed the air – until a garbage barge sailed by and blotted everything out for an hour. But then it happened. Like a message in a bottle floating on a breeze – I got a whiff of Lukie.

I locked on it like a heat-seeking missile and was rambling along at top pig speed when I got a terrifying scent. The primal alarm in my brain was screaming, *"Hot dog! Hot dog!"* – and there, in front of me, was the same hot-dog vendor from my first stroll through the park. All I needed was a second confrontation with that guy. One more sighting of a pig near a hot-dog vendor would probably mean a call to the National Guard to convert me into a basketful of weenies.

My heart told me to push on, but my pig sense said it was too risky. Ten minutes later I was back on the couch, waiting for my humans to come home. It had been quite a day. At least I had found a trace of Lukie. I prayed that he would pick up a trace of me.

CHAPTER 28

Cabin Fever in a Fish Tank

BARLEY

IF THERE WAS ever a sign that soccer season was changing to hockey season, it was the freak storm that came roaring out of Canada. It snowed like something none of us had ever seen before. Our fish tank was covered with a curtain of snow, and we all overslept. Maple, Mom, and I bundled up and rooted our way out onto the roof and had a grand time slipping, sliding, and tossing snowballs – with one eye on the roof door. Then Mom ordered us back inside, and we all huddled around the TV, eating steaming bowls of oatmeal while we watched the

Weather Channel. The city streets were blanketed in the stuff. Traffic backed up to New Jersey and Connecticut. Schools were closed, and they were telling people to stay inside unless they absolutely had to go out.

Mom got a frantic phone call from Boucher earlier than usual, saying that the hotel was full and everyone needed to be fed. Off she rushed to the kitchen after giving us the familiar chore of keeping an eye on Rumpy.

Did we ever. As soon as Mom was gone, Maple and I zipped Rumpy into her dog suit, stuffed her in the room-service table, and headed to the park to continue our snowball fight. That was big fun. Then we spent the afternoon cuddled up in the fish tank, watching cartoons. Maple made lunch, and we were as happy as clams until loud noises interrupted our snugglefest.

Murray and a pack of hotel workers came running to the roof, shouting and brandishing tools. Maple hurried Rumpy into the closet to hide, and I went out to see what was going on. I almost ran right into Boucher.

"Out of the way, tripe!" he shouted at me as he headed for the confusion.

Water and steam were shooting out of a large pipe onto the roof of the hotel. The hot water instantly melted the snow and made a little river that wound toward the stairway.

"What idiots you are!" Boucher screamed. "This whole hotel will be flooded, and my kitchen along with it." Then he spun away from the men trying to control the leak. He pointed a long, shaky finger at me. "What do you know about this? What have you been doing up on this roof?"

My first thought was that he had seen or heard us playing in the snow, and I was waiting for him to shout about our pig. That's when Mom appeared in the doorway.

"Don't you *ever* yell at my children like that!" Mom exploded. "You can yell at me all you want in your kitchen, Monsieur, but you *never* yell at my children — or anybody else's!"

I don't think Boucher had ever met Coach Mom before, and it was very apparent that he had crossed an invisible but rigid line. He immediately backed down and spun on his heel.

He turned to the group of men. "Well? What are you Neanderthals staring at?"

I heard Murray explain that something was wrong with the main hot-water line that supplied the kitchen and the laundry. Mr. Flutbein arrived on the scene, and Boucher quieted down.

They closed the restaurant, and Mom came home. A constant parade of workmen marched across the roof. There would be no more room-service-table trips to the park for Rumpy now, but at least she wasn't alone. Mom cooked for us, and we played Scrabble. Then, when the workmen were through at night, we took Rumpy out for a walk — careful to fill in her hoof prints with loose snow when we were done.

Our cozy family time lasted until the third day, and then we started to go a little stir-crazy. Up in the mountains, where it snows all the time, they call it "cabin fever." Anyway, Mom ordered Maple to clean her room. This usually melted into an argument, the only time it ever happened, and Mom would act like a drill sergeant and hover over Maple, observing the cleaning process. This time, however, Maple just scooped up her cat, said, "Yes, ma'am," and headed for her room. She was making the ultimate sacrifice for her pig, cleaning her room to be sure Mom couldn't possibly discover Rumpy's sheepdog costume.

Being the neat freak, I didn't have to worry about my room. I just read, watched Premier League soccer on TV, and played video hockey games on the computer.

Late that afternoon, I was lying in the bed next to Rumpy when a huge ray of sunshine popped through the clouds and down into the fish tank. The Weather Channel reported that the roads in the Northeast were clearing, and the airports were beginning to reopen. I wanted to show Rumpy the big TV weather map, but she was staring out the window at a flock of pigeons that whizzed by. They were the first birds I had seen in days.

"It's always a good sign when the birds are flying again," I told her. I looked out at the hot-water heater and saw no one around. The workmen were gone, at least for now.

The phone rang, and Mom answered. I could hear that scratchy voice of Boucher's through the receiver. Mom told us the kitchen was back open, and some big VIP who had been sleeping in an airport in Canada had just arrived at the hotel. He was in desperate need of fresh croissants, so Mom tied her hair in a quick knot, donned her apron, and went down to work—but not before inspecting Maple's room and giving her a "job well done" kiss on the cheek.

The thick gray clouds that had covered the city were breaking apart, and patches of blue could be seen off toward New Jersey. We knew the snow days were over, and it would be back to school tomorrow. In truth, like Mom, we were all ready to return to our regular routines, but we still had one more afternoon with our pig. I clicked off the TV and scratched Rumpy on the head. "This might be it, old girl," I said. "I think I hear room service calling."

CHAPTER 29

A Prisoner of Plumbing

Rumpy

City living was testing me.

Just when I had all my ducks in a row and was able to seriously begin my search for Lukie, Murray was back on the roof, and I was back in the closet. This time the whole boiler conked out. A major repair meant a new procession of plumbers, electricians, hotel workers, and the ever-nosy Boucher. Our once-quiet and secluded fish tank had turned into a miniversion of Grand Central Station. Mr. Flutbein offered to move Ellie to another hotel while the repairs took place, but we all knew that was out of the question because of my presence. We had no choice but to stay and wait it out. I was under house arrest again.

Bleak, gray days gave way to yet another storm, but this one just dumped an ocean of rain on our heads. Barley had school and his Red Bulls Academy, Maple had extra sewing to do, and Ellie was busy gearing up for the approaching holiday season. It seemed that my only friend in the world was the chubby but cheerful weatherman on TV, and even he was starting to sound unhappy. Now I understood why they called the storms "pockets of low pressure." I was feeling both: low and pressure.

The sky remained that shade of gray humans paint their warships, and it was again void of birds. They obviously had better sense than humans and had taken wing to warmer climates.

If this pig had wings, she would do the same.

New York had slowly overwhelmed me — and I had just about lost all hope.

CHAPTER 30

There's a Diva in the House

Barley

I WAS NOT happy about Rumpy's condition. She hated being stuck indoors, but something else was bothering her. I knew that talking to Mom about it would only stress her, so I kept it to myself. Maple and I were just fine, but Rumpy — as you know by now — was family as well. It was like having two happy children and one unhappy one.

Maple brought it to my attention that there were pet psychologists in New York, and we thought about sneaking Rumpy to one of them. Unfortunately that would involve giving out our names, address, and phone number. Bills would only form a trail that would lead to our fish tank. Boucher would have no trouble tracking down our pig.

We were at a loss about what to do. In the meantime, I had overheard Murray telling the crew on the roof that although they had been working straight through since the boiler blew, on Sunday there was a big VIP checking in, and security wanted no workers on the roof that day. I couldn't wait to tell Maple and Rumpy. We would roll the next morning as soon as Mom left for work.

When the sun finally rose, we were ready to move. As we descended, the fresh air seemed to exhilarate our pig. She raced down the stairs, slashing the air with her snout as she picked up all the scents of the city.

We followed our now-familiar plan and dashed through the storage room to the hidden table. Maple helped Rumpy get her hooves through the holes as if she were trying on a new pair of shoes. I did my usual hall patrol and returned with the dirty breakfast dishes we needed.

I peeked inside the table. "All set?" I asked.

Rumpy wiggled with excitement, making the dishes above rattle.

"Whoa, big girl," Maple added.

Since our last trip out, Maple had lined the box with a bit of carpet to make the escape vehicle more comfortable for Rumpy. We had also modified the peephole, enlarging and covering it with reflector tape on the outside so Rumpy would have a better view. The only problem with the box under the table now was the thickness of our pig's winter coat. It was a tight squeeze, but Maple and I agreed it was worth it.

Maple checked the first leg of the trip to the elevator while Rumpy and I waited for the "all clear" signal.

"Let's go," Maple whispered happily from the first corner.

We were off and rolling. Maple was about ten yards in front of us, and although the escape vehicle maneuvered like a grocery cart with a bad wheel, Rumpy had come to master steering anywhere she wanted to go. She could move surprisingly fast, slow down at a moment's notice, and even spin it around. It was like watching a mini–carnival ride.

Maple slipped ahead to check out the final turn before the elevator, and we were just about to start the last leg when her hand poked around the corner like a traffic cop's, signaling me to *stop*.

Someone was coming. This was not unusual. It was

part of the drill. Rumpy knew to position herself against the wall next to a room door. I always had a soccer magazine in my back pocket, and I would pull it out and act as if I were a typical self-involved New Yorker heading for an elevator.

This time, Rumpy made her move to the nearest door, and I brushed past the table to join up with Maple. I smelled trouble before I even got there.

The vile traces of Turkish-cigarette smoke came from only one source — Boucher. Suddenly I heard the crackle of voices coming from walkie-talkies. Could it be the police, too?

Maple and I did an abrupt about-face and headed back past Rumpy's table, hoping to get to the nearest emergency exit. We didn't make it.

"Stop!" I heard Boucher shout, and we did. We were quickly surrounded by four very large men in black suits with guns on their belts and headphones in their ears. *Uh-oh.*

The Hunchback from Hackensack stood among the men. He was talking with a tall, skinny man dressed in jeans and a long fur coat — obviously not an animal lover. One of the big men spoke into a microphone on his lapel. "Hold the package. I repeat, hold the package." Something told me he wasn't the FedEx guy.

"Do you know these kids?" the skinny man snapped at Boucher.

The chef clearly did not like the man's condescending tone, but he was nervous. "They live in the hotel. They belong to my help."

Help? What a jerk. Mom was one of the main reasons the restaurant was so popular. I started to get hot under the collar and had a brief fantasy of grabbing the table, accelerating Rumpy to ramming speed, and sending Boucher on an unscheduled flight back to France or New Jersey or wherever he came from. However, this was not the time or place to defend my mother's good name.

"Well, get them out of here." In a nasty voice, the skinny man added, "I told you this passageway from the elevator to the Presidential Suite was to be sealed and cleared, especially of pesky little fans. Royal T has no contact with *anyone* in this hotel. What about those instructions? Did you not *comprehend,* Monsieur Boucher?"

Whoa. I looked beyond Boucher and saw Maple mouth the words "Royal T!" So that was who was checking in. Royal T was a former child star on the Disney Channel who had blossomed into one of the biggest pop stars in the world. I knew she was one of Maple's favorites, and I had seen her videos. Maple said she didn't sing that well, but her outfits were outrageous. She had taken to dressing in wigs and long dresses from the old days, which were ripped and cut in some pretty revealing places. I didn't know much about Royal T, but I did know that her boyfriend was the star rookie goalie for the New York Rangers. I wondered if he would be coming to see her.

Recoiling from his tongue-lashing by the man in the fur coat, Boucher snarled at us. "You must leave here at once!"

"At the Grammys, Royal T wore a House of Wu dress! How cool is that?" Maple cooed.

"Who said that? Who mentioned her name?" the skinny man shrieked. The men in black suits pointed at Maple. "Out of here. N-O-W!"

The guys in black weren't cops. They were bodyguards for the young diva. As they made their way toward us, they were followed by an odd procession of hotel workers who were rolling a big, round awning down the hallway. It looked like one of those tubes the players run through at the beginning of a football game. It was very strange to have one in the hallway of a four-star hotel.

Two of the men took up positions on either side of us. They stopped right next to the room-service table and began inspecting the dishes. *Uh-oh.*

Please, Rumpy! Try to be cool, I prayed.

"What is *that* doing here?" the skinny man yelled.

Boucher immediately shouted at one of the hotel workers to get rid of the room-service table, and the next thing I knew, we were being escorted to the stairs.

Rumpy was moving at high speed in the opposite direction.

CHAPTER 31

A Roomful of Room Service

RUMPY

I MUST SAY that although the room-service table was hard to maneuver, I had come to master steering it on my unscheduled trips to the park. Now it was like a runaway go-cart as I moved my feet as fast as I could down the hallway to keep from being run over by my own escape vehicle.

Everything went so fast. Amid the clamor of the rattling dishes above my head, I only had a moment to catch a glimpse of the shocked looks on the faces of Barley and Maple as I whizzed by them. I wound up in a roomful of room-service tables just off the kitchen, where several busboys were removing the dishes and cleaning the tabletops with disinfectant. It almost made me sneeze, but somehow I held it back.

As I caught my breath from the mad dash down the hall, I could hear all the noise coming from the kitchen. Every now and then Ellie's cheerful drawl rose above the din of a dozen different languages that were being spoken at once. I could hear her, but she couldn't help me. If I gave away my hiding spot, she could be fired.

To add to the misery of my confinement, I was surrounded by the succulent smells of fresh-baked bread, simmering sauces, and steaming vegetables. I was getting hungry — *really hungry*. As I reveled in the scents and watched the action out my window, my survival instincts fortunately kicked in to show me the very dangerous, even life-threatening, situation I was in.

My table was in a line of tables, and as room-service orders were put together, each table was filled and whisked away to waiting diners. This was not good — because whoever tried to put an order of pancakes or a cheeseburger into the warming oven of my table would be met with the rump of Rumpy. I could just imagine the hysteria that would cause in the kitchen.

Now I was *really* starting to sweat – because my table was only two from the front of the line. With my luck, once I was captured, I would be taken to Boucher, who would send me right to that dungeon filled with chilling carcasses. I would be dressed out with an apple stuck in my mouth and probably fed to Royal T's bodyguards.

As I was envisioning my own demise, I felt the table moving. Oh no – this was it. But I was moving backward, away from the front of the line. What was going on? I saw the line of tables disappear, and soon I was around the corner. Then, through my peephole, I saw Barley's face.

Tears streamed down my cheeks. I had been rescued!

Barley and Maple steered me down an alternate route back to our hiding place, then covered me with a tablecloth and sped me up to the fish tank. I was never so glad to see my four-star cell.

"You must be starving," Maple said, and pulled a frozen pizza from the freezer. Twenty minutes later, I was stretched out on the couch with a pizza in my belly and my two best friends beside me. I wasn't even annoyed by Syrup, who was coiled on the pillow next to my head. I was just glad to be in the fish tank and not in a box or an oven.

The kids told me the story about how they saw Royal T. As they had been roughly escorted along the hallway, down the stairs, and out to the street, a huge limousine had pulled up, and Royal T got out. She was dressed like a French queen in the era of Louis XIV, but she was a lot smaller than she looked on TV, even in nine-inch heels. There were paparazzi everywhere, and she waved once to the cameras, not to her fans. Then she disappeared into the hollow awning, which snaked through the lobby of the hotel to the elevator, down the hall where we had been spotted, and right to the door of the Presidential Suite, where she was now lounging.

"I am not a big fan anymore," Maple said. "You don't treat your fans like that."

As a pig somewhat familiar with fame, I couldn't have agreed more.

CHAPTER 32

A Pilot to the Rescue

RUMPY

THE FOLLOWING week was not a good one for me. After Royal T's party, the boiler-repair brigade returned to the roof. The family went back to their respective busy lives, and I went back to the couch. At first, I was just cranky, but then I got depressed. It wasn't the workers who were weighing on me; it was my own failures. They were piling up like dirty laundry. I had failed to keep out of the way, I had failed as a loving pet, and, most of all, I had failed to find my brother. I decided it was time to quit endlessly sniffing the wind for traces of Lukie. And it was time to quit hiding. I was coming out of the closet, and I was going home to Tennessee. I needed a break.

I decided to have one last walk around the roof. Frankly, I didn't care who saw me, or if I got caught. I was done hiding. Heck, if they found out a pig had been living for weeks on end in one of the most elegant hotels in New York, it would surely become a hot story or even a front-page headline in the tabloids, with a photograph of me being led out the revolving door in hoof-cuffs. Lukie would be bound to see that, and the more I thought about getting caught, the more I liked the idea – but then what would happen to Ellie and the twins?

I regained my senses and decided to remain hidden, but I was still taking a break. All I needed was one last look at the way out of town, and then I would hit the streets and head south. Sure, it was a crazy idea, but I had heard stories about dogs that had walked across the country after being left behind at a rest stop on the interstate. If a dumb dog could walk halfway across the country, a pig could get to Tennessee. I would just smell my way back to Vertigo.

I carried my Lukieball with me to the front door of the fish tank and left it there. I was done with it. I couldn't believe that the men working on the boiler did not see me as I walked outside into the freezing wind. If the Butcher happened to show his twisted face, I would attack him, viciously sink my teeth into his skinny butt, and leave them there until uniformed men stormed the roof, pried my jaws apart, tied me down, and threw me into a transport van. It would dump me far away, where I'd be left in exile or made into sausages.

But that didn't happen. Although I almost wanted to get caught and release my anger on somebody, nobody saw me, even as I climbed up on that scary icy ledge to get my bearings. The wind howled, and I shivered.

As usual, the street was filled with strangers. They were trapped inside this loveless city, but not me. Not anymore.

Suddenly I slid. Now I was much too close to the edge. That was when I heard the voice. "Don't jump," it said, and I struggled to keep my balance.

"WHOA DERE, sweetheart," a crisp voice snapped from nowhere. "Jumping could be hazardous to your health, not to mention dat of the poisens you might squash like pancakes down dere. We can't let you do dat."

Two pigeons dropped from the air above and landed right beside me. In an official tone, the first one said, "Not often dat we see your kind up here, ma'am. We're the Pigilantes. You know about us, right?"

They were the pigeons, *my* pigeons — that squadron I had chased and wanted to meet for so long! I was surrounded by my pigeons! I was so happy to see them.

"Lady, like I told ya already, we can't let you do dis."

"Do what?" I asked. I was shivering as I tried to get a foothold.

"Jump," the pigeon replied.

Despite the cold, I began snorting and laughing. I guffawed so hard I almost slipped off the ledge. "I'm not trying to kill myself. I'm trying to find my brother."

"Looked like you were about ta break da law, so you got some 'splainin' ta do. Anyways, we got ya blocked in . . . for your own protection."

It was true — four more pigeons hovered in the air just below, blocking my view with their feathers. I had to admit they were impressive, with their matching wings and aviator helmets. They looked very informed and sure of themselves — comforting, too, since I was stuck on the ledge.

I told them everything. I explained how I used to

be so popular back in Vertigo, and now I was just an outcast city pet. How nobody had warned me that I wouldn't be welcome in New York, and how ashamed I had been of having to hide. I described how my very own humans had gotten new lives and how I had failed to find Lukie, my lost brother. Just saying his name made me suddenly start sobbing so hard I couldn't catch my breath.

The Pigilantes shook their heads and looked away politely, waiting until I got a grip on myself. One hovered nearby, extending his wing to divert the flow of my tears from the ledge to keep my precarious footing dry. Then the squadron leader landed gingerly on the gutter, inches from my face.

"Captain Frostbite, at your service," he said, introducing himself by his call sign. He went on to explain that, like me, he was not from Manhattan originally but had learned to live here. He had been carrying a message from Greenland and had been blown off course by a winter storm. He had come to like the city and the duty he performed. "New York is a big and sometimes frightening place, ma'am. And I don't want ya ta take dis da wrong way, but you're not da only pig in town. Dere's three or four we know of dat keep outta sight. And dere's one exactly like you. We fly over dat pig every now and den. Maybe he's your bruddah."

Frostbite's words made my heart jump. I longed to see his eyes, to know if he was serious, but my footing was too shaky for me to spin around. All I could do was try to keep my balance.

Half the squadron immediately landed around my feet and began pecking and pushing the ice off the ledge. The remaining pigeons stayed near my head and directed my feet in reverse until my hind legs found stability. I was so grateful, but I didn't know what to say. There *was* a pig who looked just like me in New York City!

Once I was safe and had caught my breath, Captain Frostbite continued his story. "Mind you, nobody suspects dat your look-alike is a pig. He's out dere every day in da middle of tings, in one locale or anodder. But he dresses for da job, so to speak. Seeing from above, we always know it's him. But doze people 'round him don't have a clue — he's a cool cucumber, dis guy. Dey smile and nod when he passes, and he nods right back. Tirty minutes ago, we buzzed him at da zoo."

An excitable gray pigeon broke in. "Yeah, when da polar bears get all laddered up about da heat, dat pig, he chills 'em right out. Den da seals, dey love ta tell him jokes, so when dey see him comin', dey start wid da stories, and he's laughin', and dey're clappin', and . . ."

Frostbite broke in, waving him off to the side. "We been keepin' an eye on ya since ya got here. It ain't hard, since ya live in dat fish tank dere."

"But I thought all the birds had gone south?" I said.

"No, not us." Frostbite laughed. "We're just hard to see against da gray sky. We ain't snow boids. We are always on duty. Speakin' a which, it's my duty to 'splain da rules here. Let's start wid fallin' objects. See, ma'am, dey are a hazard for us boids — and for da walkers and drivers and city morale. Where ya lived before, dere probably wasn't deez skyscrapers, but here, we're on patrol 24-7, just keepin' da airspace clear. So stay back from da ledges, and we'll tell ya more tomorrow. We got lotsa weenies to roast up here, but . . ."

Captain Frostbite saw the horrified look of the other Pigilantes and realized the offense he had just uttered. He stuttered for a few seconds, but then he regained his composure as any good commander would. It was simply the way flyboys talk, and besides, I was too happy with the news about Lukie to take anything these birds did or said as an insult. "Excuse me, ma'am. I sincerely apologize for dat weenie ting."

"Apology accepted," I said immediately.

The captain continued, "I just wanted ya ta know dat me and da fellas here will discuss da matter at hand, and findin' your bruddah will be a priority patrol for dis squadron. Right, fellas?"

All the Pigilantes nodded their heads in agreement.

The captain continued, "I would suggest that maybe yuz postpone dat trip ta Tennessee for a while and continue ta dwell in your present surroundings. You kin use dat telloscope of yours to better advantage now dat ya have air reconnaissance along."

"You saw that?" I asked, interrupting the captain.

"Sista, we got a boid's-eye view of everyting dat happens in dis city. Anywayz, while you and doze kids figger a way ta get ya back on da street, we will find your bruddah."

Then he saluted me and signaled the other Pigilantes. His army launched from the ledge in unison and circled over our heads.

"Ma'am, we got a pig ta find. Ciao for now." With that, Captain Frostbite catapulted into the sky and took up his position at the head of the Pigilante squadron.

I watched their air show until they were out of sight, and the sun broke through a ribbon of clouds to the east. At last, my days were getting brighter – much brighter.

IT WAS RAINING the next day, but I was one upbeat pig. I had a head full of new ideas, but before I could begin putting them to work, I trotted into the kitchen and actually had an early breakfast with the family. Everyone noticed the new bounce in my step, and Ellie even made me a fresh-fruit salad with pineapples that had just arrived from Hawaii — *hula-hula!*

CHAPTER 33

Something to Fit the Occasion

Barley

The last week of October began with two big news items.

First, the boiler was fixed, so the workmen left the roof. This meant we could resume Rumpy's walks outside. Royal T and her entourage had packed up their protective tunnel and security team and moved on to another town, but after our last close call, Maple and I weren't ready quite yet to resume the room-service-table missions to the park.

The second big announcement came from Maple and involved the big school dance on Halloween night. The grand prize for the best costume was tickets to the House of Wu Fall Fashion Show and lunch with Karen Wu. Needless to say, all of Maple's attention was on that costume, and she had no time for much else.

As for Mom, high season in Manhattan was in full swing, and Flutbein's was booked solid for months. Of course Boucher was taking all the credit, as he had done during Royal T's self-imposed isolation; for a week, it turned out, she'd been sitting in her room ordering Mom's pastries while she watched her boyfriend play hockey. The Hunchback from Hackensack's behavior never seemed to bother Mom like it did us kids. She always believed that one day her good work in the kitchen would produce its own just dessert.

And if all that wasn't enough activity, another blip on my radar screen was that the Red Bulls were playing D.C. United for the Eastern Conference Championship the day before the costume contest. I had e-mailed Dad, reminding him of his promise to take me, but I hadn't heard from him. Just to be sure, I had a backup plan. I had made friends with one of the trainers at the Red Bulls Academy, and he had promised me two tickets if I would help him get a reservation for his mother at Flutbein's. Mom worked out some kind of trade-off with the maître d'. That was kind of how New York worked, and I liked it.

With all that going on, we still had to take care of Rumpy. When she wasn't working on her costume, Maple had pulled together a Plan B to get Rumpy back to the park.

"Rumpy. Wake up. We have something to show you," Maple whispered in her ear. Rumpy twitched as if she were having a nightmare.

"No, no, no," I said. "No more room-service tables, Rumpy."

Her eyes popped open; she stretched her short legs and wiggled her head, which was her sign to snuggle. Maple and I surrounded her on the couch.

"We figured with it being Halloween week in New York, everybody is probably going to start showing up in all kinds of outfits. This would be the week to spruce up that sheepdog look," Maple said. "Come on, Rumpy. Come see what I've got to show you," she coaxed.

Rumpy rolled off the couch and followed us to Maple's room.

"Ta-da!" we exclaimed together. It was Maple's finest sewing accomplishment yet. She had redone the dog costume. It was so real that it almost looked alive, sitting on the bed. I could tell Rumpy was pleased.

"When we get home from school, we will have a fitting, and by the weekend, you should be free to roam the park again," Maple said.

We kissed her on the snout and headed off to school, talking about our costumes. As always, Maple kept her outfit a secret, but this year, I had a little costume idea of my own.

CHAPTER 34

A Stitch in Time

Rumpy

I COULDN'T HAVE been happier to spend the day in the fish tank with my new escape outfit. I stayed in Maple's room, just examining the costume for a long time. I don't know what kind of dog I was becoming, but I knew I had seen a similar character on one of the thousands of cartoon shows I had watched since coming to New York.

Maple had done the work of a genius. The costume was so limber that after about thirty minutes working with it, I was able to get in and out of the dog suit by myself in seconds. The mask was comfortable, and I could see normally. I kept taking it off, putting it back on, and prancing in front of the mirror, practicing my "dog moves" – which doesn't take much. I wasn't even hot in the costume. Maple had sewn air vents under the legs and into the rump. The dog suit was a sensation with ventilation.

Sometime in the afternoon, I was awakened by the sudden slamming of a door, and Ellie's voice called for me. I abruptly came to my senses and dragged the costume under the bed, then climbed back on top of the mattress and faked a recognizable sleeping position.

"Poor thing, I ran out of here so fast, I forgot to feed you." Ellie used her chopping skills, which equaled – or bettered – any sushi chef's I had seen on the Food Network. In minutes, I had a fresh vegetable platter in my bowl.

"In France, they call this crudités," she said as she scratched my head and put the bowl on the floor. "Got to run, girl. See you later." She disappeared out the door again.

I was chomping on the last stalk of celery when I heard a tap at the window. I was overcome by fear. I was about to bolt for the closet, but first I peeked at the big window. Fear turned to excitement when I saw Captain Frostbite and several of the Pigilantes perched on the windowsill. I nudged the window open, and a big rush of wind gushed in, bringing the pigeons with it. They lit on the sofa.

"We have news," Captain Frostbite reported. "I tink your bruddah was spotted today, but I wanna confoim it foist. No need for you ta be takin' risks for no reason."

The words were music to my ears. My head was swirling. I had been living on hope for so long that even a possible sighting of Lukie made me dizzy. I didn't know whether to snort for joy or cry. What I did know was this: Captain Frostbite and the Pigilantes had pecked my path from that icy ledge. I knew they were birds I could trust.

"What should I do?" I asked.

"We got it on a good source dat your bruddah, Lukie, was spotted by da elephants in da zoo," he explained.

"The zoo in the park?" I asked.

"Dat would be da one. Just cool your hooves till weez gets a confirmation, and den we can come up wid a plan."

I told them about the dog costume that Maple had made for me and about the twins' idea to use Halloween weekend as a cover to get me out. Frostbite seemed to think that was an excellent idea because it also gave them enough time to run down the lead on Lukie.

Through the open window, a scent crossed my radar. It was the kids. They were on their way home from school. I told the Pigilantes, and they headed for the window. They reminded me that the unwritten rule about this kind of stuff was very strict: *No humans could know*. With that, they ducked through the crack in the window and took off for the park.

I watched them disappear behind the trunk of an oak tree and said a prayer to the pig gods to send me a sniff of my brother's whereabouts.

CHAPTER 35

Let Them Eat Pizza

BARLEY

BACK IN Tennessee, when Halloween rolled around, Mom would run me to the local Wal-Mart to pick out some cookie-cutter, store-bought outfit — just in time to go trick-or-treating around Pancake Park. Maple, as expected, made her own costumes. Over the years, she was everything from Barney to Barbie.

That seems like ancient history now, because once Maple came to New York, her costume creations leaped to a different level. If you thought my sister's work on Rumpy's escape suit was good, you won't believe what she did for our first Halloween in Manhattan.

Once Maple finished Rumpy's outfit, she went back to working on her costume for the school dance. She was determined to win that trip to the House of Wu. One day, after class, Maple was waiting for me at the entrance to Barton, which was unusual. She told me she had some errands to run and wanted me to go downtown with her.

Our first stop was a large gray building near Times Square. It was the House of Wu, and it was lined with display windows filled with mannequins showing off their stuff. Maple had made pilgrimages to the windows ever since we had come to New York, but every visit, she was as excited as she was the first time. She looked like a kid let loose in her first candy store, and I finally had to grab her arm and bring her back to reality. "What are we doing, other than looking at clothes?" I asked.

"You'll see."

She led me back to the subway station, and our next stop was Greenwich Village. The street was crowded with costume stores like you have never seen. We just walked around, looking at outrageous costumes and all kinds of masks, capes, fake body parts, alien eyeballs, gowns, goblin heads, and a thousand other things. I was starting to get excited, but then I began looking at the price tags. Man, New York was expensive!

"What are we doing here, Maple?" I asked. "We can't afford this stuff."

"Oh yes we can," she said with a sly smile and produced an envelope packed with twenty-dollar bills.

"Oh my God, you robbed a bank. Mom is going to kill you!"

"Noooo, Barley. I e-mailed Dad and told him how much we were looking forward to our first Halloween in New York — and that I wanted to design a really special outfit that might get me lunch with Karen Wu."

"A large bowl of guilt soup served up to the absentee father," I said.

"Exactly," she replied, not missing a beat.

"I e-mailed him about the play-offs and haven't heard a word," I said.

"His selective memory at work," Maple replied. "I must have caught him in one of his fat moments, because I got a Halloween card and a check for three hundred bucks — and it didn't bounce. If he doesn't come through for you on the tickets, I will buy you some. Now, let's shop!"

And that is what we did. You would have thought Maple was designing a dress for J. Lo to wear to the Grammys, but knowing my twin sister the way I do, I knew this was not a haphazard spree. She checked off everything on her small red notepad.

"What are you making?" I asked.

"You'll see."

I have to admit that I kind of got into it, too, and I started my own costume project as well. I decided to go to the dance as a miniature spaceship. I cut two large sheets of cardboard into a saucer shape, and then I snipped a hole out for my head and covered the cardboard with aluminum foil. Finally, I put on my hooded hockey sweatshirt and painted a third eye in the middle of my head. I wrapped my waist and legs with strands of Christmas lights and stuck a battery in my pocket. To top it off, I converted a set of bunny ears into antennae and stuck them on my head.

Maple's room looked as if a nuclear clothes bomb had gone off. Piles of fabric and zippers and spools of thread were everywhere, but the costume was hidden behind a black curtain Maple had hung in the corner. Rumpy was a constant observer, stretched out on top of the bed. Syrup had taken up a position to prevent any curious bystanders from getting a peek. Since Mom had been using her few spare hours after work to help Maple, that left only me to be guarded, and I wasn't messing with that cat.

Finally, a few days before Halloween, Maple was

ready for her costume debut. She, Mom, Rumpy, and Syrup were all gathered behind the curtain, giggling and gabbing, and then classical music began playing from Maple's iPod. Out stepped Marie Antoinette in a green velvet dress with pink-and-green flowers running down the puffy sleeves, and she held . . . *her bloody head in her hands!*

Poking out of the collar of the dress was Marie's blue-gray neck and the stem of her spinal cord. I stared at the head.

"Let them eat pizza!" Marie screeched.

Rumpy snorted, and Mom was rolling on the floor, laughing.

"Maple, is that you?" I asked.

"How dare you address the queen in such an informal way! Mind your manners, or you will join me at the guillotine."

I took about a hundred photos from all angles and then helped Maple out of the costume. Over dinner, she took me through her whole process of construction. It was remarkable. There would have to be something unbelievably good and freaky to beat her out at the contest.

Speaking of freaky, Mom told us the story that the mother of the mayor of New York City had been in the restaurant, and Boucher had escorted her around. It seemed the mayor's birthday was coming up, and she wanted to surprise him with a dinner party Saturday night at Flutbein's. She had specially requested one of Mom's famous cakes that she had heard so much about from her friends. Mom was on the mayor's radar! How cool. New York is like its own country, and the mayor is a very popular and powerful person in this town. Boucher, of course, promised to grant her request, laying layer upon layer of schmooze about all the preparations *he* would be making. Thinking of him was almost enough to spoil our dinner, but not quite. As Mom dished out our lobster omelets, she sighed. "I don't know how much more of that suck-up, stuck-up sausagehead I can take."

Mom gasped and looked at Rumpy. "Oh, honey, what was I thinking? I am so sorry for using the *S* word." She went over and gave Rumpy a kiss on the top of her head. "And what are you going to dress up as, Miss Rumpy?"

We froze in place, stiff as statues, and then Maple regained her composure. "I'm working on something," she said.

"Do that, honey," Mom told her. "It would be fun to sneak the old girl out of the hotel for a while."

Maple and I must have looked shocked.

"Just remember, you two, I was a kid once." Mom smiled.

CHAPTER 36

Blood Is Thicker than Cotton Candy

RUMPY

THE OBSESSION with the creation of the Marie Antoinette costume was just the diversion this pig needed. After the news from the Pigilantes about sighting Lukie, and Ellie's news to the kids that I could go out, I was on pins and needles. My big break was finally coming, and I could hardly wait. I also watched the Doppler radar on the local news. The chubby weatherman kept talking about the perfect weekend ahead for trick-or-treating.

Meanwhile, the hotel was a circus all day Friday. Along

with the daily routine of arriving and departing guests, the preparations for the mayor's surprise dinner added everything from serpentine salesmen to SWAT teams, banner hangers to bomb dogs. The kitchen was a war zone, and Ellie was covered in flour both day and night. She was starting to look like the cake she was attempting to bake for Saturday night.

One really good thing about all this activity was that Boucher actually had to work, too. That kept him out of the dining rooms and hallways, according to Barley and Maple. They had been scouting his moves in preparation for my big adventure of leaving the hotel for our Halloween excursion.

Early the next morning, before anybody was awake, Captain Frostbite tapped on the big picture window. I nudged the smaller vent window open and let him in. "Have you made contact with Lukie?" I asked excitedly.

"Not exactly, ma'am," he answered. "We are confident, doh, dat wit da messages we have carried all over da zoo and da city, he will find out dat we need ta tawk ta him."

I told Captain Frostbite of our impending plan to go trick-or-treating with the kids in my new disguise.

"Brilliant!" he squawked. "Dat makes da plan much easier to carry out, now dat we don't havta rescue you offa dat roof." He paused for a moment, rotated his head in a circle, and then said, "I tink dis is what we do." He proceeded to lay out a plan in military terms.

First, I was to go trick-or-treating Sunday with the kids before their big dance. Then, as soon as we were clear of the hotel and got to the park, I would give the twins the slip and join up with Frostbite. We would search for Lukie while a couple of pigeons kept an eye on the kids. I would join back up with the twins – hopefully with Lukie by my side – by the end of the evening.

Captain Frostbite approached the plan with utmost seriousness. "The important and difficult ting is for da kids not to know your intentions ta leave 'em. It will be hard, but we havta take our best shot at findin' your bruddah."

I knew he was right. I felt really bad about skipping out on Maple and Barley, but finding Lukie was the one thing that would make life in New York complete. Barley had his sports, Maple had her designing, and Ellie had her cakes. All I had was a ragged football with a fading face.

I told Captain Frostbite I was in, and I wouldn't tell a soul.

WITH ALL the anticipation, Friday passed slowly. To keep my nervous jitters to a minimum, I played with my Lukie-ball for the better part of the day. That afternoon, when

Maple came home from school, I was subjected to my final fitting – with a few pin pokes and alterations. That night, before Ellie went down to the restaurant for a staff meeting in preparation for the mayor's dinner, it was my turn to take the runway. Barley set the blaster by the sofa and pushed the button. "Who Let the Dogs Out" blared from the speakers, and out I came from the bedroom. After my prance through the living room, though they could never quite decide on my pedigree, I was pronounced stunning as a dog – from the hair extensions on my tail to the faux diamond–studded collar around my neck.

It was early Saturday morning, only one more day until Halloween, and tonight was the mayor's birthday dinner. My day began when a bright ray of sun lit up the whole living room. As I slowly opened my eyes, the fish tank was surrounded by a perfect blue sky, and I let out a big sigh of relief. I lifted myself off the couch and took a long stretch. The apartment was unusually quiet. We had all stayed up late, modeling for one another, and the kids were still asleep. I had heard Ellie come in, but I had no idea what time that was. There were none of the usual sounds of Ellie in the kitchen making breakfast, but a scent in the air made me shudder.

I had completely forgotten the treats Ellie had promised to bring home the night before until a perfume of caramelized sugar made its way to my snout. I knew what was in the kitchen – cotton candy, one of my favorites. I leaped off the sofa as if I had just consumed a triple espresso and headed lickety-split toward the treasure leaning next to my bowl in the kitchen corner. Just as I was about to devour that large, pink triangular swirl, my morning treat was shattered by a frantic tapping at the window. When I looked over to see what was going on, the entire Pigilante squadron was crowded on the sill. They looked frantic.

I was diverted from my route to the bowl and headed to the window. Before I could nudge it all the way up, Frostbite ducked into the opening. "Your bruddah was spotted in da park only five minutes ago. It's time to make a move if ya wanna catch him."

"But I'm not ready!" I protested in shock.

"Few of us ever are. If ya wanna try and catch him, we havta go *now*."

I thought for a second about my beautiful breakfast treat and then about Ellie and the kids – and all the fear and concern they would feel if I was missing.

"Rumpy!" Frostbite said in a stern voice.

What could I do? "Blood is thicker than cotton candy," I muttered to Frostbite and went to suit up.

I sneaked quietly into Maple's room, trying not to look at the innocent expression on her sleeping face. My costume was lying under her bed. I felt like a home-wrecker, but I had no choice. I carefully carried my costume back to the living room, where I managed to put it on with the help of the Pigilantes. It reminded me of that scene from *Cinderella* I had seen on TV when she is getting dressed for the ball. I just hoped I didn't turn into a pumpkin this Halloween Eve.

"Quite impressive," Frostbite said with a salute. He wished me luck and told me they would meet me at a statue in the park.

Figuring out how to escape the hotel without detection wasn't an option. I just had to work it out as I went. I slipped through the door of the fish tank and headed for the elevator. The door opened, and I went in. I knew that on any floor, the elevator could open and the Butcher could step in and discover me. I tried to put the idea out of my head, replacing that thought with visions of Lukie.

Next thing I knew, I was in the lobby. Not hesitating for a moment, I went into "stuck-up uptown dog" character, raised my nose, and proceeded across the marble lobby as if I owned it. The sound of my hooves clicking on the floor set a natural rhythm as I followed a trio of perfumed ladies gliding toward their waiting limousine. When Freddy held the door, I thought about joining them, but a better option appeared I spotted a dog walker out on the sidewalk.

For those of you who aren't familiar with the term, in big cities, people make a job out of collecting dogs from owners of apartments and hotel guests. They take the dogs collectively for a walk around the park to let them get some air and do their business. Well, this dog walker looked like one of those stagecoach drivers in an old Western movie. He must have had about a dozen leashes attached to a dozen different breeds of dogs. There were golden retrievers, dachshunds, Great Danes, poodles, and Pekingese, and they seemed to be dragging the dog walker past the front door, barking and yipping all the way.

Freddy saw the dog walker coming and immediately nodded his head toward the side double doors. I made my move. I rushed from the elevator, sped through the revolving doors, and joined the pack of dogs passing by. Nobody even paid attention to the fact that I had no leash. A hotel guest added a Westie to the pack. I stayed with the dogs to the corner, where a policeman held up traffic so we could cross.

Now I was in the park. I veered left as the dog walker

and his herd walked right, and no one batted an eye. I was concerned that two dogs on the corner would spot me as an imposter under my faux fur, but the Afghan rudely looked away while the mountain dog beside her whistled and winked admiringly as I passed. The humans seemed completely oblivious, so I assumed a rhythmic canine swagger and headed for my rendezvous with the Pigilantes.

CHAPTER 37

Halloween Comes Early in New York

Rumpy

It was still a day early, but it was the weekend, and people were already out in the park in costumes. To my delight, many humans had dressed their pets for the occasion. This made my walk to the zoo even less noticeable.

I have to say that dogs are really given carte blanche in New York. Any mangy mutt with a collar and tags gets red-carpet treatment. It does not go unnoticed by the rest of us four-legged creatures.

I found the statue that Frostbite had described, and the Pigilantes were there, perched on the arms of Simón Bolívar. Even they didn't recognize me at first until I gave a familiar snort. Then they swooped down and landed in a circle around me.

Some kids nearby dressed as bunny rabbits were throwing peanuts, but the Pigilantes paid them no mind and cooed their reconnaissance to me. A pig disguised as a possum had definitely been spotted near the elephant cage in the zoo, and word had it that he was searching for another pig disguised as a dog or a room-service table.

"That's me!" I yelled excitedly.

"Dat's you, sistah," Frostbite said with glee. "We would love ta do an aerial sweep of da park, only ting is we got an emergency over on Coney Island. You can head over to da zoo and start looking. We will come back and give ya air support as soon as we are free. Good luck!" Frostbite said. He saluted, and then they left for their mission.

I was just about to go to the zoo when – *wham!* – I smelled him. It had been soooo many years, but the scent was just as strong as when we were piglets. My nose locked in, and I followed along.

My heart was about to jump out my throat, and I did my best to conceal my excitement. I attached myself like a devoted dog to the nearest group of humans as they chatted and walked down the path. I kept up the pace right at their heels so we appeared to be together.

I peeled off from the humans when I saw the sign that

pointed in the direction of the elephant exhibit. Lukie's scent got even stronger. I was greeted with howls, growls, and hoots by the animals on the other side of the bars. It seemed that the larger the animal, the more helpful it proved to be. The elephants were the first to confirm that Lukie had been by their exhibit no more than five minutes ago. I was beside myself.

I had been focusing completely on Lukie, so I hadn't noticed that the chubby weatherman's morning forecast of sunshine had been off. It started to rain, and the canaries weren't the only creatures to go into a dither as the first drops fell. The humans joined the frenzy as the rain started coming down in buckets, and they ran for shelter. I continued alone toward the seal pool.

The elephants said the seals knew everything that went on in the park. They must have been right, for as I headed to the pool, Lukie's scent got stronger. I was tempted to let out a huge roar; if he heard it, he would immediately recognize my hog call, but I held my tongue for fear of creating a panic in the park.

As I trotted along, solo, in Lukie's direction through the quickly forming puddles, my costume and I were soaked. The wind began to howl and bend the branches of the tall oak trees. The sky grew darker overhead. I should have known it was an omen. As the drops turned into a deluge, water began to pour through the eye openings of my costume, and my vision blurred.

The reaction to thunder in the animal world is like the human reaction when a jet breaks the sound barrier at treetop level. When the boom came, it instantly ignited my survival instinct — not only to the terror of the thunder but to something else in the air that I couldn't quite understand. The stampede of rain-soaked tourists was on, and in no time the caged animals retreated from their open areas to their caves, and I was left alone.

Believe me, I wasn't humming "Singin' in the Rain." The storm had temporarily drowned out Lukie's scent, and I, too, sought shelter from the storm. I spotted a deserted wooden bench and strained to squeeze myself under it, but water trickled right through the seat, continuing to soak me, and it was getting colder.

Then, as quickly as the rain had started, it suddenly ended. The dark, ominous cloud moved away from the park, and the sun reappeared. I wiggled free from under the bench and stood to shake the wetness off, but I found the costume had acted like a sponge and had soaked up a good part of the deluge.

I returned to where I had been standing when the skies had opened up, but now I was a much soggier, heavier pig. A group of humans were trying to get organized as they pulled off the yellow plastic ponchos that had been distributed by the overly efficient tour director. She folded her umbrella, blew her whistle, and resumed the tour.

People in New York don't seem to waste a minute. I fell in behind them again, trotting toward the seal pool, where I hoped to reacquire Lukie's scent. As I heard the happy bark of a seal, I noticed my hooves were flashing like signal mirrors, reflecting the reappearing rays of sunlight. But that wasn't the worst of it. Maple's costume had begun to *shrink*. It was shriveling up in odd segments and shifted sideways on my back. I was looking less like a dog with every step and more like a you-know-what.

"Cochon!" a voice behind me growled as a knife blade whizzed into sight. I instinctively leaped, but it grazed my snout. I stumbled, then rolled into a hedge. I froze in silence just ten feet away from my attacker. I had heard about muggers and city gangs — Ellie was constantly warning her children to be watchful. But who would pull a knife on a *dog*?

I couldn't believe what had just happened, but instantly I figured it out. That putrid stink of Turkish tobacco, garlic, and wine belonged to only one person — Boucher. When I caught sight of him, he was stooping down in his long black coat to wipe my blood from his blade on the wet grass.

CHAPTER 38

I'm Not a Sausage — I'm an Animal

RUMPY

TO MY HORROR, after attacking me, Boucher did not flee like the criminal he was. Instead, he slid the knife under his coat and shoved aside a city gardener. He grabbed a set of gas-powered hedge trimmers — the kind with giant scissor arms on the end. While the gardener shrieked, Boucher cranked up the trimmer, and the scissors swept back and forth rapidly, like the jaws of an alligator devouring every branch of the hedge in which I was hiding. Boucher was carving the shrubs like a madman and was now only yards away. When he reached the end of the hedge, I knew he would find me.

Things were not looking good. The shrill whine of the hedge trimmer, combined with his furious voice, tangled my thinking. I searched desperately for another hiding place, knowing he would twist the story and claim a hero's reward for saving the city from a delusional pig dressed in a dog suit, running madly through the shrubbery.

The Butcher would explain that such a wild, rabid creature had to be put out of its misery for the common good. Blades slashed closer and closer as he screamed, *"Le cochon aujourd'hui . . . le saucisson demain!"*

As people began to shout at him for destroying the hedge, he yelled out, "Stay back! There is a wild, rabid pig in here!" He kept warning the shocked crowd, as if I might bite or injure one of them. Meanwhile, the gardener had taken refuge under a picnic table.

My options were running out. I could either charge the Butcher and become the crazy pig he claimed I was or try my luck in the open field and make a run for it in the opposite direction.

I was about to dash to the seal pool when I heard Boucher cursing above the noise of the machine. He was frantically swatting the sky with his free hand. The Pigilantes had returned, and they were dropping their "bombs," which splattered all over his long black coat with perfect accuracy. The Pigilante raid provided just the distraction I needed to slip out of the bushes without being seen by the Butcher.

As I made my break, some of the young zoo trainers came out in brightly colored wet suits. Carrying beach balls and buckets of sardines, they stepped onto a large rock in the middle of the seal pool as a chorus of hungry barks erupted from the delighted seals. This ritual was a favorite of the crowd, and everyone rushed to the pool, forgetting about Boucher and his hedge trimmer. Hiding in the crowd, I took a breath and bolted like a cannonball, though my stride was restricted by the costume's increasingly tight fit.

Just as I hit a decent speed, I was distracted by the sight, dead ahead, of a passerby casually flicking a lit cigarette behind him. It landed in a box of rags and cleaning fluid under a nearby work shed just off the bike path. In a matter of seconds, the dry rags were aflame, and they quickly ignited the storage shed. Peeling painted letters on its side read CAUTION: FLAMMABLE LIQUIDS.

I put on the brakes when I saw an old lady seated on a nearby bench with her back to the inferno, feeding several squirrels, totally unaware of the impending danger. She was dressed, I must say, even worse than I was, in a long shaggy coat and a hat with giant plumes that trailed all the way down her back. She looked like a Christmas candle about to be lit.

I veered from my escape route, took the end of her coat in my teeth, spun her around so she could see the flames, and then dragged her to safer ground. Just then, a park police car arrived on the scene. Without a backward glance, I resumed my flight, having no idea how strange I looked or that a crowd had gathered around the old lady. All I was thinking was how to get back home to the security and safety of my fish tank and family.

When Flutbein's loomed ahead, it gave me the strength to keep running until I finally limped through the service gate. Inch by inch I sneaked past hotel workers, security guards, and hall maids. I retraced my old room-service escape route to the roof, hoping somebody would be home to let me in.

I was in luck. I could see the glow of the TV in the living room and the image of SpongeBob dancing around on the screen. I scratched the door and banged against the glass.

Syrup popped her head above the couch, and Maple stood up and looked my way. I must have been a sight in my tattered and bloodied costume. I was cold and shivering, and my heart was pounding with fear. Blood still trickled down my nose.

Maple rushed to the door and opened it. "Rumpy! Where have you *been*? Mom and Barley are . . . oh no!" she screamed. "You're hurt! What happened to you?"

I couldn't even look up at her. I was *soooo* ashamed of running out on them. I just crept slowly toward the sanctuary of my spot in Maple's closet, but Maple stopped me in my tracks and made me lie down. She was already administering first aid to my cut as she patted my head and cleaned and bandaged my snout.

Well, there was still one person in the world who loved me.

The phone rang. She got up to answer it, leaving me alone on the floor in her room. I heard her tell Ellie that I was home, but my thoughts turned to the predicament in which I found myself. Would I ever see Lukie again? Would the Butcher hunt me down and attack again? How could I communicate to any human what he had tried to do to me? It was too much to think about, and I just wanted to crawl back into the closet, snuggle next to my Lukieball, and worry about what was coming next. I didn't have to wait long.

CHAPTER 39

Just Dessert

Barley

FALLING DOMINOES always fascinate me. You usually see them on some "believe it or not"–type TV show that features a video of a large hangarlike room filled with all imaginable kinds of curved and looped ramps, bridges, ladders, waterwheels, and windmills, and about a jillion dominoes stacked neatly and precisely next to one another along a track. Then some guy, usually wearing a lab coat and thick horn-rimmed glasses, is lifted up in a bucket crane to the beginning of the trail. He gently taps the first domino, and the chain reaction begins. The dominoes fall in speedy succession. One topples, and the next thing you know, the whole room has collapsed. It looks so smooth and controlled and graceful on television, but in real life, I am here to tell you it's a different story.

I guess what first started our family dominoes falling was Rumpy's disappearance. I had planned to take advantage of the good weather that Saturday to go to the park and play in a pickup soccer game, but I was diverted into a search party by Mom. The city was all abuzz with playoff fever, and about half the guys on the field that morning were going to the game that afternoon. Of course, I would rather have been playing soccer, but I knew I had to look for Rumpy.

To make matters worse, I still hadn't heard from my dad. I had made the swap with the trainer for his tickets, which were in the nosebleed section, but they were tickets all the same. I just hoped I would have someone to take with me to the game. If my dad pulled a no-show, then I was going to ask one of the guys in the pickup game to go. Just as I was about to give up looking for Rumpy, I saw Maple running toward me. Maple never ran. Something was wrong. I raced to her as fast as I could. She told me that Rumpy was back home but that our pig had been attacked by somebody.

She also told me that Mom had said Boucher hadn't shown up for work that morning. "Do you think it's just a coincidence that Rumpy and Boucher both disappeared today?" she asked.

I didn't know how to respond. The dominoes were falling. As we were about to cross the street on our way back to Flutbein's, a huge procession of fire trucks came screaming through the park and stopped on the edge of the Great Lawn. Smoke was rising up above the trees.

When we first moved here, the constant wail of sirens really bothered me, but after a while, I stopped paying attention. This time, Maple and I could see it was something big, and we went over to check it out.

Somebody said the mayor's mother had almost burned alive in a freak fire, but she had been rescued by an anteater.

"Well, that's New York for you," I said.

"There's too much weird stuff happening here," Maple added. "Let's go home and take care of Rumpy."

As we came around the corner toward the revolving doors, the huge limo that had originally brought us to the hotel pulled up at the curb. Out of the back door popped my dad, wearing a Red Bulls jersey. He held a smaller one for me. "Surprise!" he said. He gave me a big hug, and before he could grab Maple, she took his hand.

"Come with us," she said. On the way up to the fish tank, we explained what had happened. Rumpy was sleeping when we checked on her. Before we could offer any ideas about the situation, Maple said, "We will be fine. Just keep your cell handy. You guys better hurry, or you will miss the start of the game." What a cool sister.

Dad gave Maple a hug, and then we were off to the game.

The dominoes were turning into a landslide.

CHAPTER 40

Anteater on the Loose

RUMPY

I DON'T KNOW how long I slept. The care and feeding I had received from my human had certainly brought my physical self back around, but the mental scar of being sliced by the Butcher was still very fresh indeed.

In a fitful nightmare, I'd been trapped back on the icy ledge inside the room-service table while Boucher tried to connect gas pipes to it, turning it into an oven with me inside. Then the dream changed to a serene hill behind our house in Vertigo, where the whole family was gathered for a picnic, but I wasn't anywhere in sight.

The ring of the phone woke me up and brought me back to my hiding place in Maple's closet. When I peeked out at the day, I could tell it was early evening by the color of the sky in the west above the park. I studied the airways for any signs of the Pigilantes; those birds could certainly explain to me what had happened in the park. They were not around.

"Rumpy?" Maple called to me with a large question mark in her voice. "You have to see this. Please come out."

I could hear her talking to Barley on the speakerphone. From what I could make out, he was at the soccer match, and something playing on the JumboTron at the stadium had made him call Maple. He was shouting above the roar of the crowd.

I had behaved pretty badly toward the kids, and my shame about that more than my fear of the Butcher had me curled up in Maple's closet. I owed them a lot, so out I came.

"Good girl," Maple said as she led me to the living room.

SpongeBob had been interrupted by a newsbreak, and the mayor's face appeared on the screen, haggard and distraught. He was in Central Park, standing in front of a fire engine with a dozen cameras pointed in his direction. The mayor was making a plea to the people of New York for help with a personal matter. He went on to explain that a hero had saved his mother's life and then vanished without recognition. As he spoke, some shaking footage played of an old lady being dragged from a flaming bench by a weird-looking creature. The mayor described the creature as an anteater, which the police and fire department were trying to locate. The mayor closed by offering a reward to anyone with information about this noble hero.

"Hmmmm," Barley's voice mused over the noise of the crowd in the speakerphone. "Does that anteater look familiar to you?"

Maple looked at me. "Very familiar indeed."

They were doing that twin mind-meld thing, and I knew exactly what they were thinking. Then Maple smiled at me and said into the phone, "Barley, I think we have just bought this anteater a one-way ticket off this roof forever. Tonight is the mayor's birthday dinner, remember?"

Barley told her Maple to keep me hidden, and he and Oliver would come right home after the game. Then we would all go down to the hotel lobby and tell the mayor the whole story — right in front of Boucher, Mr. Flutbein, the camera crews, and the entire population of New York

City, which would be the perfect time and place to ask Mr. Flutbein to end the exotic-pet ban at the hotel.

"Perfect," Maple said with a smile. Barley hung up and SpongeBob reappeared on the TV, but Maple and Syrup had their eyes focused on me.

"That was one clever old anteater, wasn't it, Rumpy?" Maple asked.

I snorted with joy, even though my snout hurt. I knew that through the bizarre events that had just transpired, I had found a completely new way to find Lukie. The mayor was my key. I had saved his mother; now he would help me find my brother.

CHAPTER 41

It's Not the Avon Lady Calling

RUMPY

JUST AS I WAS about to doze off, the front-door buzzer rang. Maybe it was the mayor, and my prayers had been answered earlier than planned. Since he was such a smart man, it probably didn't take him long to find out that the pig who saved his mother actually lived upstairs on the roof of Flutbein's Hotel, where he and his mother were about to have dinner.

Maple went to answer the door, but even before she reached it, my snout picked up the all-too-dangerous, familiar stench of Turkish cigarettes, garlic, and wine. Syrup dashed by me and bolted under the bed. I heard Maple squeak, "Monsieur Boucher! What a surprise!"

I peeked out as best I could from Maple's room.

In the doorway, Boucher loomed over her. He was wearing a bloody apron and held a brightly wrapped gift under his arm. The smile on his face was sinister. "Ah, Mademoiselle, your mother's very busy tonight, and she wanted me to check on you . . ."

Listening to his sickening effort to charm Maple, I was torn between wanting to launch an immediate attack on him and trying to compress myself like an octopus so I could squeeze into the farthest corner of my hiding place.

"Mind if I smoke?" he asked as he lit up a cigarette and slithered into the living room. "Where is your brother?"

"He and my dad are on their way back here from the soccer game."

"You have a father? Ha! I thought you two were hatched." He bellowed at his rude joke.

I was starting to get steamed up at the thought of this butcher bullying little Maple, but she was a cool customer. "They just called from down the block," she told him calmly.

Boucher tried to move farther into the apartment, but Maple stood in his way. His eyes scanned the living room and kitchen.

"Really?" he said, exhaling a large cloud of putrid smoke. "I heard on the radio that the game was tied. They were about to start the penalty kicks. Doesn't seem like a game any real soccer fan would want to leave, does it?"

Maple didn't take the bait. "No, they should be here any second." She was trying to act relaxed, but I could detect the fear in her voice.

I wasn't going to let this go on much longer. I stretched my neck farther out to try to get a better view.

"Tell me," he said, now dropping the phony sweetness from his voice, "when did you get rid of that swine and get a family dog, in keeping with the policy of this hotel that *forbids* exotic pets?"

I knew where he was going and got ready to attack.

"You know, that was my idea," he bragged. "I convinced Mr. Flutbein that the only place for exotic animals in this hotel was on a serving platter. Did you know that in China they eat dogs?" he said, followed by that sickening laugh. "You're devoted to your pet, I feel sure . . . but since I also love animals, won't you show it to me?" he asked.

For a moment, Maple didn't respond, but then she calmly said, "No, Monsieur, we have no dog. Just a cat."

"Then what is *this?*" Boucher hissed, and yanked something out of his jacket. It was not the knife he'd used on me but a handful of 8 x 10 photographs. I inched toward the doorway and could clearly see images of the kids in their ASPCA shirts, strolling through the park with me on a leash. There were also several shots of the room-service table, one of me in the lobby with the dog walker, and finally a close-up of me in the park near the hedge where he had attacked me.

"I can fire your mother and send you and your brother to reform school. You have broken the law. The dog you claim not to have is a *pig!*" he screamed.

I was now on high alert. I knew any minute I might have to give my life for Maple, and I was ready to do it.

"You think I only know about food?" Boucher ranted. "No! Boucher knows a few other things, too . . . *Number one,* canines do not have hooves like lesser creatures do. *Number two,* swine are stupid and vulgar and sufficiently unclean to contaminate whole cities . . . and *number three,* it is irresponsible — not to mention illegal — to conceal a hog in a hotel in Manhattan!" The Hunchback from Hackensack took a swig of whiskey from a flask in his coat. Then he lapsed into French. "*Et quatre, cinq, et six, les enfants* who commit this crime routinely go to prison!" Blue veins rose steadily in the pale sides of his face as he raged away. "You thought no one was watching when you took your pig for a stroll? Wrong!" he boomed. "I am too clever to be deceived by children. You see, I was just waiting for the right moment." He pulled a cell phone from his coat and stabbed away at the numbers. "The police are swarming around this hotel, looking for any person or any pig that might present a potential threat to the mayor . . ."

"You can't call the police without talking to my mother!" Maple cried.

"Of course I can! I am the head chef of Flutbein's Hotel," Boucher snarled. "And as for you ill-mannered, spoiled brats, you will be taken away to a dark cell where large spiders are happiest. Your idiotic mother will believe you ran away and will die quite soon of heartbreak – and I will take all the credit for her marvelous desserts. But before then, I will *dine* on your *pet*." The vision perked him up. "So . . . how do you feel now, Mademoiselle?"

Sobbing, Maple just stood there.

This was it. Now was the time to charge the Butcher and hit him with all my speed and weight. Hopefully I would cripple the fiend. Then I would squeal so loudly the whole city would be on our roof in seconds – cops, Pigilantes, Barley and Oliver, Lukie, and every person and creature in the whole wide world. I knew they would all hear my cry for help. But just as I was about to heave myself in the direction of the murderous Boucher, I was overcome with a hypnotic aroma. It made my legs weak, and my head started spinning.

Boucher had pulled the brightly colored wrapping off the gift box he was still holding under his arm. He tore off the plastic seal and placed the box on the table. "Since you have decided not to tell the truth to your mother's employer, I'm afraid you must watch the beast die."

I immediately knew the box contained my favorite food in the whole word – chicken fingers, the heroin of hogs, steaming and juicy and sizzling.

Boucher continued, "Hypnotized by the scent, your pig will be drawn to my hand." He reached into his coat and pulled out an even deadlier device than his knife – a giant hypodermic needle, which he raised up to the light. Out of the end of the needle, he forced the first few drops of what had to be some kind of poison.

Wild-eyed, he leered at Maple. "It will be instant death by injection." Then he whispered in an almost comforting tone, "Don't worry, I am not going to send your precious pig to the Beanie Weenie factory." He moved back toward the table and put the box of chicken fingers on the floor. "No, no, no! Next week, you will see your pet on a national magazine cover." He reached for the fruit bowl. "Like this!" he screamed and jammed an apple into his mouth. He ripped a bite from the fruit and spoke as he chewed, spitting pieces of apple onto the floor. "And its eyes will be sewn shut – the centerpiece of my next feast!"

Maple was paralyzed with fear.

Then Boucher began to sing, "First injection, then convection, then I roast it to perfection . . ."

CHAPTER 42

Follow Those Pigeons

BARLEY

D.C. UNITED had come out on fire and scored a stunning goal in the opening minute of play. Then, for the ensuing one hundred thirteen minutes, my dad and I joined the other forty thousand soccer-crazed New Yorkers in watching a scoreless match. At the start of the game, Dad had all the enthusiasm of a fanatical Red Bulls fan, but by halftime, his team spirit had fizzled. He told me that watching a soccer match was like watching paint dry.

Suddenly, the Red Bulls seemed to sense the desperation of the situation and took a cue from the name stitched across their jerseys. They came roaring down the field with just over two minutes to play. The crowd immediately felt the energy shift, and they jumped to life as well. People all around us were shouting and stomping their feet, and then everyone started chanting in unison. Against all odds, our top striker, Miguel Miguel, had positioned himself in the box for a last desperate shot. I wasn't the only one who saw him slip in. An entire stadium filled with Red Bulls fans and the whole United defense watched him, but it was too late. Out of a cluster of United and Red Bulls players, the ball suddenly crossed into the box and ricocheted off the back of a defender. Miguel Miguel rocketed toward the ball, and for a moment it seemed suspended like a little planet in orbit. Then he launched a header into the corner of the net. We were tied and going into overtime.

I don't know how I heard the cell phone in my jacket ring in the melee that followed the goal. It must have been that "twin thing" at work. Somehow I knew it was Maple, but what took me completely by surprise was what I heard coming through the phone.

My sister was panic-stricken, and in the background I could hear the hissing shouts of Boucher. It was obvious that the Hunchback from Hackensack had discovered

Rumpy and was threatening Maple. The Red Bulls would have to win without us.

I plucked Dad from the celebrating throng and told him Maple was in trouble. We tried calling Mom, but I knew she'd have her hands full with the mayor's dinner; her cell phone just took a message, and the phone line to Flutbein's was one long busy signal.

Somehow the soccer and traffic gods seemed to sense our need to rescue Maple and Rumpy. We sped across the George Washington Bridge in ten minutes and then saw the clogged lanes of the West Side Highway and flashing lights in the distance. Dad finally got through to Mom and told her to get to the roof with the police. When I heard him say, "That creep better not lay a finger on my little girl!" I knew that he meant it.

As our taxi crept along, I took in a strange sight — a flock of pigeons that seemed vaguely familiar was circling the cab. When we stopped in front of a red light, they landed in formation on the hood of the taxi, and the lead pigeon pecked on the windshield. They were trying to tell us something.

"Follow those pigeons!" I told the cabdriver.

He looked at me like I was crazy, and then he looked at my father.

"You heard my son. Follow those pigeons!"

CHAPTER 43

An Unexpected Order

RUMPY

FROM THE MOMENT the Butcher arrived, I had anticipated the worst. I had just been waiting for the right time to make my move, whatever that turned out to be. I wasn't expecting the chicken-fingers trap, and it almost worked — but I wasn't ready to be turned into bacon yet.

The moment called for a little sacrifice on my part if I were to rescue Maple, so I pretended to be under the lure of the chicken-finger spell. I dropped to my knees while the Butcher prepared the injection.

"Now to clear a path to my storage cellar for the soon-to-be carcass," the Butcher told Maple. "Lots of company for you in the cellar, piggy-piggy."

He walked to the front door and opened it. "This is your route to your new life — I mean *death!*" he sneered and then turned back and grabbed the box of chicken fingers. He held them out with one hand while he clutched the giant syringe with the other. "Come to papa," he hissed.

I looked up at Maple, and I could see she had her hand on the cell phone, but she was afraid to pick it up. I squealed at the top of my lungs, and it provided just the distraction she needed. I watched her touch the speed dial, and then I went back to my acting.

"You can't do this!" Maple shouted.

I pretended to be under the Butcher's spell and sniffed the air with my snout. I waddled out from Maple's room and slowly staggered toward Boucher, acting as if I had guzzled two quarts of beer. I didn't care if he found his mark with the needle — I would charge him at the last minute and knock him all the way to Jupiter.

A split second before I was going to charge — *wham!* — I smelled him. Even through the chicken fingers, scent-mails were coming through the open front door. I knew it was Lukie, and he was close.

Suddenly the Pigilantes were on the sill, pecking at the window. The Butcher looked up to see what was making the racket, and that's when I saw the room-service table come barreling through the front door.

I didn't have to imagine what was propelling my old escape vehicle, for the scent of my long-lost brother was getting stronger. The creaking of the wobbling wheels made the Butcher turn, but it was too late. The table rammed into his legs and sent him flying — along with the chicken fingers and the giant syringe. The room-service table veered right and crashed into the sofa. When it turned over, out popped the beloved face I hadn't seen in years. It was Lukie. He had found me.

My immediate thought was to cover him with kisses, but the danger of the moment wouldn't allow it. Lukie climbed out of the wrecked table and lunged at Boucher, who lay in the middle of the floor, clutching his knee and cursing in French.

Suddenly a herd of humans stampeded through the door, led by Ellie. Barley and Oliver followed. Maple ran to her mother's arms, and Barley and Oliver joined Lukie in hovering over the Butcher. Our family was followed by Mr. Flutbein, the mayor, and a dozen policemen. Guns were drawn and pointed our way. I didn't know if they were going to kill the wild pigs, the mad Frenchman, or both, when the mayor boomed, "Where is the anteater?"

"Mr. Flutbein, I was removing this swine from the hotel, according to our policy, when the pig attacked me. Shoot it. Shoot it now!"

"He's lying!" Maple shouted. "Boucher is an evil man, and he tried to kill our pet pig!"

"What pig?" the mayor asked with a puzzled look. "We are looking for an anteater." He held up a photo of me in my costume.

I walked from behind Lukie's protection and into Maple's room. I came back with the sheepdog head held gently in my mouth.

"I think we have found our anteater," one of the policemen said.

I rushed back to Lukie's side, and we started spinning around like horses on a merry-go-round, rubbing and snuggling.

As the police dragged the Butcher off in handcuffs, Barley and Maple joined in the pile.

CHAPTER 44

Icing on the Cake

Rumpy

There is a song sung by a great human named Aretha Franklin called "Respect." I used to dance to it back in Vertigo when I entertained the locals. To tell the truth, I didn't actually listen closely to the words. What I loved was the beat and particularly that place Ms. Franklin would sing, "Sock it to me, sock it to me, sock it to me," over and over again. Be you human, animal, vegetable, or microbe living at the bottom of the ocean, if you can't dance to that part of the song, well then, you need to move to another part of the galaxy. Humans do have their moments, you know, but they often make things much more complicated than they really are. We animals fight over territory, but nothing we have ever done has started a war. Sometimes I think it must be hard to be a human with a brain that can at times create such wonder and at other times wreak such havoc.

I had come to New York expecting the whole human world to fit into mine, and I was kicked out-of-bounds like one of Barley's explosive crossing shots on the soccer field. I admit I whined and got depressed, but even in my times of hopelessness, I still knew in my deepest heart that somehow, some way, I would see my brother again. The gods of good fortune had smiled down on me, and because of a random act of kindness, my world came together the way I had always dreamed it would. I didn't have to hide, wear a dog suit, or stuff myself into a room-service table anymore. Not only had I found my brother but along the way I had earned a little "respect" — which in my humble, piggish opinion is all any of us really want anyhow.

At first, when Maple and Barley saw Lukie, they assumed I had a boyfriend. But Ellie chewed on her lip for a moment and said, "I can hardly believe it, but that is no boyfriend — that is Rumpy's *twin brother*. I remember him from when they were babies. See how much they look alike?" Everyone made a huge fuss, and I twirled and twirled so Ellie would understand that she had been absolutely right.

A few hours after my ordeal with the Butcher, I was perfectly refreshed and enjoying my newfound celebrity status. E-mails and text messages spread the word like wildfire throughout the hotel about the heroic you-know-what living in the fish tank on the roof. And — get this — Lukie and I were invited to have dinner the next evening with the mayor and his mother. I was happy.

THE NEXT morning, it was Halloween at last. The whole staff applauded me like a hero when Barley and Maple took Lukie and me to the park. Twins leading twins. It was about all you could hope to have.

I knew that Maple and Barley now understood the reason for my strange behavior over the past few weeks. When we got to the Great Lawn, they hugged Lukie and me, and then they climbed above us on a big rock where they could keep an eye out for strangers but could give us privacy.

There was so much to discuss. First, Lukie told me how he first saw the Pigilantes in Battery Park. He had been on a field trip with kids from the School for the Blind, teaching them how to follow him down a sliding board. Once he got the word I might be in town, he had made his way from Greenwich Village, where he had been living, to "Canada," his nickname for uptown Manhattan.

I wanted to stay there all day and night and talk to Lukie, but in New York, there never seems to be enough time. Catching up with my long-lost brother would have to wait until after our dinner date with the mayor and his mom. The mayor's birthday dinner had been postponed from the night before so that he could take care of his mother. He rebooked the dining room for the next night, and Mr. Flutbein and Ellie made it happen. Ellie was exhausted but thrilled to be working without the shadow of the Hunchback from Hackensack. There would be plenty of time for walks in the park.

Mr. Flutbein had insisted that I be taken to the hotel spa for a deluxe treatment. There — to the amusement of most, and the shock of others — I was bathed, massaged, and coiffed like an Upper East Side matron. They even manicured my hooves and applied a topcoat of frosted pink. While I was in the spa, Maple was putting the finishing touches on her Halloween costume. As soon as dinner was over, we would head to Barton Academy and the big costume contest.

Dinner unfolded like a yummy Fruit Roll-Up. Mrs. Bloomfield, the woman I had saved in the park, still wore her dreadfully large hat and fawned over me and Lukie all evening as the cameras clicked away. She insisted on feeding me the salad course one leaf at a time, interrupting the cherished lettuce flow with multiple hugs and squeezes. The paparazzi ate it up. When you're a star, you have certain duties . . . and posing graciously is at the top of the list.

The mayor beamed to see his mother so happy. I beamed to see my brother next to me. Mr. Flutbein brought Ellie, Oliver, and the twins by to greet the mayor. Ellie, of course, had excused herself and had retreated to the kitchen. With Boucher on his way to jail, she had been made temporary head chef by Mr. Flutbein. The packed dining room was buzzing with conversations and a lot of glances at our table. Then, quite elegantly, the mayor tapped his glass, silenced the crowd, and rose to his feet. He retold the now-familiar story of how I saved his mother. There wasn't a dry eye in the dining room when he called for a toast to his mother — and *me!* Everybody stood and raised a glass as the band struck up "New York, New York."

I could smell the cake and floral extravaganza before they even entered the room. Seconds later, Ellie and her staff surrounded a way-too-familiar room-service table, and they guarded the floral centerpiece on it as if they were Secret Service agents. The kids clapped and whistled as their mom passed by, and Ellie gave them a wink.

Just before the cake was rolled to our table, Ellie signaled to one of her sous-chefs. He pulled a string, and the top of the floral centerpiece opened up. Out flew the Pigilantes in perfect formation, thrilling the breathless guests. Frostbite took them around the room, swooping down and back into the crowd in a dazzling little air show before he led his squadron out an open window.

The mayor's mother led the room in singing "Happy Birthday" to her son as the headwaiter rolled in Mom's famous volcano cake and began to slice generous portions for the guests. Mrs. Bloomfield and I were presented with the first two pieces.

It was quite a New York moment, and as I sat there in the packed dining room of the fanciest hotel in New York City, with my adoring family and my beautiful brother by my side, feasting on volcano cake, I was beginning to *really* like this town.

CHAPTER 45

A Taste of Show Business

Barley

THINGS MOVE fast in the Big Apple. As I look down from the fish tank, winter appears to be losing its grip on good old Central Park. March is a lamb, not a lion, this year, my first spring back in New York.The skeleton-like branches of the trees are begging to sprout green buds, and the early-morning joggers aren't dressed like Eskimos. Pretty soon I will be on the Great Lawn, trying out my new cleats in the fresh green grass. I can hardly wait.

It seems as if we have lived in this city for years. In many ways the park below reminds me of the view from the porch of our farmhouse back in Vertigo, but

Tennessee now feels like ancient history. I think we have all become New Yorkers.

This has not been a hibernation winter for the McBride family, and a recap might be in order. I guess I better start with the aftermath of Monsieur Boucher's attempted attack on Rumpy. Of course the local gossip rags had a field day with the story of our pet pig's rescue of the mayor's mother and Boucher's violent behavior – but it only lasted a few days, until the next outlandish, headline-producing event came along, which involved Royal T's hockey-playing boyfriend punching a photographer. In this town, there is never a long wait for splashy news. Mr. Flutbein did fire the Hunchback from Hackensack, but Boucher did not go to jail. My mom was not seeking revenge. She stayed calm and reminded us that you have to look for some good in every bad person or situation. That is the way she handled the problem with Boucher.

First she consulted with us, and then we unanimously agreed not to press charges. Instead, we requested that the mayor require Monsieur Boucher to do eight weeks of community service. We asked that he split his time between the park zoo and the animal shelter near our school.

Two weeks into his new job, a kind of miracle occurred. Mom went by one day to see how he was doing and to bring him a slice of spinach quiche. Over lunch, Boucher apologized to her for scaring her daughter. Then, in a tearful confession that had Mom searching her purse for tissues, the Hunchback told Mom that he had grown up in a dark, depressing neighborhood in Paris. More than anything in the world, he had loved to go to the zoo and the parks, and as a child, he had wanted desperately to have a pet — any pet. But year after year, his parents would never allow it.

In some twisted way, he developed an extreme jealousy of children who had pets, and it only got worse when the family moved to Hackensack, New Jersey, where it seemed that every single child he met had at least one dog or cat. His seething resentment festered into a hatred of all animals and children. He begged Mom's forgiveness, and she accepted his heartfelt apology.

After finishing his community service, he stayed and worked at the animal shelter for the rest of the winter, and with Mom's encouragement, he attended classes to become a vegan chef. Just last week, he got a job at a restaurant in Woodstock. He finally got his first pet — actually two of them — orphaned German schnauzers from the shelter he had grown to love. He stopped by the hotel for a visit and then headed for Woodstock with his van and his new family of dogs.

Mom's job as temporary head chef at the hotel lasted only two weeks. Then Mr. Flutbein made her full head chef. The publicity that focused on Rumpy's story had increased the hotel's fame and popularity, and Mom was not one to see an opportunity and not take advantage of it. The advance wait for a table was now three months, and people came from all over the world to eat and stay at Flutbein's Hotel.

More important for our immediate family, Mr. Flutbein lifted the ban on exotic animals in the hotel and granted us permission for both Rumpy and Lukie to stay in the fish tank. If that wasn't enough to make us dance a jig, he gave us the use of an old farmhouse that his family owned out on Long Island, where the pigs could stretch their legs, roll in the mud, and get in touch with their inner-farm-animal selves, and Mom could plant her garden.

At the first chance, Mom, Dad, Syrup, and both sets of twins – kids and pigs – piled into a rented van and drove to see the farm. It was unbelievable. Lukie and Rumpy ran and snorted and dug with their snouts until they could hardly stand up. Then we had a huge family soccer game. Lukie is as nimble a goalie as his sister. Dad sprained his ankle. Maple fixed him up with a special bandage and fashioned a designer cane for him out of an ash-tree branch.

Later, Mom laid out the plot for a giant vegetable garden that she would plant after Groundhog Day, which would provide fresh vegetables for the restaurant. Maple and I found a place near the driveway where we could build a small stage to bring back Rumpy's Vertigo tango act for our new neighbors and their kids.

Meanwhile, back in the kitchen at Flutbein's, Mom didn't wait long to put her unique touch on a classic New York eatery. She emptied Boucher's meat locker, rewrote the menu, and brought a new philosophy of natural ingredients cooked by happy people in a happy kitchen environment, which instantly resulted in rave reviews of the food, decor, and service. Despite the three-month wait, hopeful diners stood in long lines running down Fifth Avenue in case of a cancellation.

Then Mom took up our idea of Rumpy's entertainment revival. She introduced "Tango Night on Tuesdays" at Flutbein's, with a top-notch couple from Argentina. I don't suppose I have to tell you who the featured closing performer was. By my count, from Christmas to

Valentine's Day, Rumpy appeared on the *Today* show, the *Tonight Show, Live with Regis and Kelly, Sesame Street,* and several European networks. Rumpy is wallowing in the glory, but I think what makes her even happier is that she is with her brother. While Rumpy soaks up the spotlight, Lukie is doing what he loves at our neighborhood school for the blind, where we drop him off every morning on our way to Barton Academy. In the evenings, we take him and Rumpy for long walks through the park, where they seem to be known by both locals and tourists alike. Every weekend, they go out to the farm.

Maple, of course, won the costume contest at Barton Academy with her Marie Antoinette outfit, and she became quite a celebrity at school—but that was only the beginning. After seeing her other designs, Karen Wu immediately offered Maple a part-time apprenticeship. Mom made sure it didn't interfere with her schoolwork, and so now, two afternoons a week, Maple designs kids' clothes for the House of Wu. They bought her the latest high-tech sewing machine and a new computer, which she uses to create all her designs—as well as to do her homework. Syrup is still her cat coat and can be seen most nights staring into the computer at Maple's latest creations.

With Flutbein's becoming the rave of Manhattan, it didn't take long for the new chef to get on the hip-restaurant radar. Gone was the "buckets-of-blood lunch bunch." They were replaced by foodies from all over who had heard about Mom's cooking. Among them were the producers of the Food Network, who told Mom they were looking for a new concept for a cooking show. That is when she asked Dad for help; new TV concepts were right up his alley.

Mom and Dad spent several weeks working together on the idea, and they didn't argue once. Whatever they were cooking up, they kept it top secret. It drove us crazy, and we tried every trick we knew to get either one of them to spill the beans about the show, but they stuck to their guns.

Dad did not move into the fish tank, as we were already a bit overcrowded, but he got an apartment several blocks away, which they used as an office, and it was off-limits to Maple and me. That was fine, though. We just liked having Dad close by. As far as living together, well, we will just have to wait and see. But it is nice to have them both in our lives at the same time.

As for me, after the party at Flutbein's, things just moved along. School was good, and of course there was always soccer. Then one morning, an announcer on ESPN launched a verbal bombshell that shocked not only me but the whole soccer world. Darryl Meacham – still my all-time soccer hero – had left Real Madrid and was moving to Hollywood to play for the Los Angeles Galaxy in the MLS. He was also talking about starring in a movie.

The story was on every sports page and Web site in New York and all over the world. It wasn't like he was the first athlete who turned into a movie star, but I just thought playing for Real Madrid was the top of the international heap, and once a Madridista, always a Madridista. I had done the math – I was twelve, and Meacham was twenty-seven – so by the time I turned seventeen and he was thirty-two, we could both be playing for Real Madrid at the same time, or maybe he would come to America and finish out his career with the Red Bulls. I was *so* disappointed.

As the headlines continued in the papers, I went to the indoor field at Chelsea Piers and kicked away my anger and frustration every afternoon. I was so tunneled in on Meacham that all the excitement at home about the debut of the TV show didn't register. It was Maple who reminded me on the way to school, and she had to ring me again when I forgot that I was supposed to meet her at the House of Wu. A car was picking us up to rendezvous with the rest of the family at the premiere, which was being held at Flutbein's.

I was still in my soccer clothes, so Maple quickly grabbed an outfit for me from the fitting room. We had yet to see the show or pick up any clue about it. All Dad would say was that the Food Network people thought it was going to be a smash hit. I didn't want to be a pessimist, but Dad had said that about everything he had ever written or produced. Mom, on the other hand, said the same thing, and Mom was a straight shooter. We could see her excitement, and this made us even more curious. But they still wouldn't tell us anything.

"You need to get over this Meacham thing," Maple said as we climbed into the backseat of the car. "You are just being selfish."

"I'm not the one who bailed," I said defensively.

"Put yourself in his shoes. He's only trying to make the most of his time as a star."

"He's a soccer player, not a movie star or an action hero," I snapped as we sped along Fifth Avenue past Rockefeller Center.

"Wrong," Maple said. "It's all the same thing. Do

you think the House of Wu would be in business if they sold the same stuff over and over again? Change is a necessary thing, and maybe in Meacham's case, he needed a change."

I didn't reply. I stared out the window as we passed a horse-drawn carriage full of tourists heading into the park. I did not like where this conversation was going. Maple was making too much sense.

The scene in front of Flutbein's fortunately brought the subject to a close. It looked like Oscar Night. All that was missing was Joan Rivers and her daughter. A long line of stretch limousines crept toward the curb, where a red carpet made a path to the street. Rows of photographers were packed behind lines of policemen, their cameras aimed at the approaching cars. One after another deposited stylish passengers.

"There's the mayor," I said to Maple, but she was fixated on the girl exiting the car in front of us. "Oh my gosh! It's Royal T, and she is *sooo* thin. Can you believe she is wearing the same Karen Wu dress she wore at the Grammys?"

I looked, but Royal T had already disappeared amid a barrage of flashbulbs. Next thing I knew, our door was open, and there was the familiar happy face of Freddy the doorman. "Now *this* is the way to arrive at Flutbein's," he said with a wink and a hand for Maple.

The crowd erupted into a cheer, and Mom, Dad, Rumpy, and Lukie scurried down the red carpet to meet us. We smiled and waved to the cameras as Freddy kept us moving past the throng and through the safety of the revolving doors.

Inside, several efficient handlers dressed in chef clothes and exercise outfits quickly led us to the main dining room. It was more packed than the night of the mayor's birthday party. The crowd applauded as we were escorted to the head table, where the mayor and his mother greeted us. We took our seats.

Mom looked gorgeous in—what else?—a Karen Wu/Maple McBride dress they had designed especially for the occasion. Dad had bought a new pair of jeans, had gotten his hair cut, and actually wore a pair of socks. Rumpy had bows on her head and tail, and Lukie sported a bow-tie collar. The lights went down, and the big screen at the front of the dining room lit up.

CHAPTER 46

Pig Out

RUMPY

WELL, OKAY, I will admit my mistakes when I am proved wrong, and I was wrong about Oliver. Back in Vertigo, when those kids barely had their father in the picture and Ellie worked incredibly hard to be a good single mom, the name "Oliver" meant "big-time loser" to me. Any reference to Oliver made me angry, and I would become particularly ill-tempered when he showed up to play the role of substitute parent.

I confess now that I actually attacked him once. He was trying to act like Father of the Year and to fit in, and

I was playing with a piece of shag carpet that I chewed on for fun. When he tried to involve himself in my game, I let him think he was welcome. Then, when the perfect chance came, I bit him on the butt. *Hard.* Now, watching myself tango on the big screen to a room filled with laughter and applause, I was going to have to eat my words. In the end, Oliver finally came through for his family, and I was an apologetic pig. It might have been Ellie's desserts that got things rolling, but it was Oliver's Peter Pan propensities that finally paid off.

Oliver got up and introduced Ellie, called for the lights to be lowered, and then rolled the first episode. The top secret show he and Ellie had cooked up for the Food Network featured Ellie talking to Royal T about what she liked to eat. Since Royal T was originally from Louisiana, her favorite meal was a jumbo oyster / soft-shell crab po'boy sandwich, fried green tomatoes, okra salad, and a giant chocolate-macadamia-bread-pudding king cake for dessert.

In the episode, Ellie and Royal T cooked the meal, and then Royal T sat down and ate it. As she dined, though, the plates were connected to some kind of a computer that flashed the number of grams of fat and calories that went into her body with each bite.

Halfway through the meal, who should sit down at the table on the screen but Darryl Meacham! I thought Barley was going to faint. The audience in Flutbein's went wild. Meacham didn't say a word. He watched Royal T eat her dream meal, and while she did so, he took notes.

When she moved her napkin out of her lap and onto the table, Ellie asked Meacham what he thought. He said that while she was eating the meal, he had come up with a soccer workout routine that would guarantee she would lose all the weight of the meal in an hour. Ellie then informed the TV audience that if Meacham's routine did indeed work, a $25,000 check would be donated to each of their favorite charities.

The live audience let out a collective sigh as the video scene then switched to Meacham and Royal T on a soccer field. She now had wires attached all over her exercise suit, and the same computer that gauged her dinner was now hooked up to a giant flat screen on the side of the field. At the sound of a gun, they went to work, music played, and a crowd cheered as Royal T went through a hellish routine of running, kicking, and diving – grinding, groaning, and sweating buckets.

As the hour drew to a close, Royal T worked frantically with Meacham's instructions, and with ten seconds left, a big o appeared on the screen. The video ended to the audience erupting into thunderous applause. The lights came up, and Royal T and Darryl Meacham walked out onto the stage in front of the screen with the name of the new show flashing behind them in large pink letters: PIG OUT.

Meacham was dressed in a tuxedo, and Royal T pulled off her black Karen Wu dress to show her slim, buffed shape in a leotard and a tight-fitting miniskirt. Ellie joined them in front of the screen with two larger-than-life checks for $25,000 written to Royal T's and Meacham's favorite charities. At that point, Ellie, Oliver, and I were called to the stage, music blared, and I led the whole cast in my tango routine. The crowd leaped to its feet and clapped in time as we danced to the *Pig Out* theme song.

We didn't have to wait for the reviews. *Pig Out* was an instant smash hit.

CHAPTER 47

Always a Madridista

Barley

I DOUBT VERY much if I would have ever met Darryl Meacham if we had stayed in Vertigo, but I was surely not acting very "New York" about it. I stood there as speechless as the Statue of Liberty for what seemed like an eternity, not able to move my limbs or my lips as I stared at my ultimate hero on the stage. It was Dad who brought him over to the table and introduced us.

"I hear you're pretty upset with me," Meacham said with a slight smile.

I wanted to run like Forrest Gump out the fire exit,

up Fifth Avenue, over the George Washington Bridge, down the New Jersey Turnpike, hang a right at Pennsylvania, and not stop till I got to the Golden Gate Bridge. It was Meacham's voice that stopped me.

"Tell you what, mate. I'll meet you in the park tomorrow morning, and we'll kick it around a bit. Seven good for you?"

I couldn't speak. All I could do was nod my head up and down.

"Seven it is then, mate."

Meacham was whisked away by a press lady to an adoring crowd.

Of course I had trouble sleeping that night. I don't know if it was sheer nerves or the can of Red Bull that Mom suggested I drink in order to stay awake for the party. In the morning, I crept out the revolving doors of the hotel. Fifth Avenue was deserted, and a chilly breeze whistled through the trees as I crossed the street, wondering what words would come out of my mouth when I got to the Great Lawn.

The sun was just peeking over the horizon, and the sky was orange around it and blue above. A few early birds jogged in the park, and I bounced my ball as I walked. It was strangely silent — no cab horns, no sirens, no yelling, no nothing. Then suddenly a fluttering above my head broke the stillness. I looked up to see Rumpy's flock of pigeons as they circled the trees and then dove in front of me. They landed in formation on the road and escorted me directly to the soccer field. I guess the word was out.

Meacham was already there. He wore a plain black workout suit and was sitting on the bench, reading the sports section of the *New York Times*. I knew that every soccer nut in the world would want to be standing in my cleats, but I had a sudden urge to turn around and go home. I didn't have time to finish the thought of fleeing because Meacham saw me approaching and waved.

"Where's your pig?" Meacham called to me as he put down his paper.

"She's not up yet," I told him.

"That's one smart animal you have there, you know."

"Yes, I do."

"I've been thinking of getting a pig myself," he said as we walked toward the Great Lawn.

I couldn't believe that I had Darryl Meacham all to myself, with the opportunity to ask him anything – How does he make the ball go where no one else can? What is it like to score the winning goal in the European championships? – and all we were talking about were pigs.

"I've read about George Clooney and his pig, Max. It seems that having a pig is a pretty good way to deal with the ladies in your life. I guess there are those who like pigs, and those who don't. How does that work for you?" he asked.

"I don't have a girlfriend. Rumpy is just my goalie."

"See? There's another perfectly good reason to get a pig. Do you think George Clooney's a soccer fan?"

"I have no idea," I replied, "but I've heard that things are very different in Los Angeles. My dad used to work out there. He says that some giant like Paul Bunyan grabbed the country by the neck and shook it like a big sack, and all the fruitcakes and weirdos landed in the bottom of the bag — and that's California." I wanted to bite my tongue as soon as I said it.

Meacham just laughed. "Well, I guess I am about to be one of those fruitcakes. Right, mate?"

He held his hands out, an indication that he wanted my ball. I tossed it to him, and we walked farther onto the field. It was empty, and he motioned for me to run to the corner as he snapped his right leg and sent the ball in a missilelike trajectory out ahead of me. Somehow I managed to catch up with it and kick it back.

"I thought a lot about this California move, whether it was the right thing to do and how pissed off the fans in Europe might be. But I can tell you two things, Barley McBride," he said as he kicked the ball back to me. "It's true, I did it partially for the money. You know these legs won't always be as strong as they are now, and I think I have earned the right to secure my future. But I mostly did it for the adventure. I grew up a poor kid in Liverpool, and I still can't believe my lucky stars that all this has come my way. Would you turn down an opportunity to star in a movie?" he asked.

"I see your point."

"Besides," Meacham continued, "Europe was ready to find a new me, and I wanted to go to a place where I could still be the old me. And although I will now be playing out there among the 'fruitcakes,' as you call them, I can tell you one more thing, Barley McBride. In my heart, I will always be a Madridista. And you may be the next me."

With that, he unzipped his warm-up jacket and dropped it into his gym bag. He had on his Real Madrid jersey with the famous number "5" on the shoulder. At the same time, he pulled another jersey out of the bag and tossed it to me. "That's the last real one left. Put it on."

I slipped the jersey over my head, trying to digest what had just happened, and when I could see again, there up on the big rock near the Great Lawn sat Mom,

Dad, Maple, Freddy, and Syrup. Walking out onto the field were half a dozen hotel workers in a variety of soccer clothes. They were dressed to play. Right behind them, Rumpy and Lukie waddled toward the opposite goals. Rumpy was wearing a very decorative fiberglass mask that Maple had made for her after the attack to protect her scarred snout.

"I think we've got a game, mate!" Meacham said with a grin. Then he yelled, "Madridistas forever!"

"Madridistas forever!" I echoed, and we ran together toward the field.

"Let the games begin!" Maple yelled from the big rock.

I let out a huge whoop and laughed.

"Swine not?"

About the Author

For decades, Jimmy Buffett has delighted readers and music lovers with his highly imaginative songs and stories. Born in Mississippi and raised in Alabama, Buffett splashed down into the world of fiction in 1989 with *Tales from Margaritaville,* the longest-running bestseller of that entire year. Two subsequent novels, *Where is Joe Merchant?* (1992) and *A Salty Piece of Land* (2004), topped the bestseller lists, and with the publication of Buffett's autobiography, *A Pirate Looks at Fifty* (1998), he became one of only nine writers to have claimed the #1 bestseller spot on both the fiction and nonfiction lists of the *New York Times.* Among his many professional accomplishments, he has recorded more than forty albums, most of which have been certified gold, platinum, or multiplatinum.

About the Illustrator

It was serendipitous when longtime friend Helen Bransford showed Jimmy a short manuscript and photo-illustrations based on her pet pig, Forkie. For years Helen's friends had been entertained by her funny stories about her adventures in New York City, hiding the family pig in an upscale hotel. Now Bransford, an author and artist, presents readers with an unforgettable pig accompanied by a tale that only Jimmy Buffett could invent.

ALSO AVAILABLE IN PAPERBACK

A Salty Piece of Land

A novel by Jimmy Buffett

"A tangy tale . . . fresh, fanciful, finely imagined. . . . Very possibly Buffett's best work to date."

— Kinky Friedman, *New York Times Book Review*

"It's great fun. . . . You'll feel as if you're somewhere else — a place where a swim in cool water and a breakfast of banana pancakes with coconut syrup will cure any hangover." — Lynn Andriani, *People*

"An entertaining Caribbean romp. . . . The twists and turns of Buffett's characters make this book a brisk page-turner." — Steve Morse, *Boston Globe*

"It goes down like a piña colada: smooth and sweet."

— Michael Harris, *Los Angeles Times Book Review*